I0822639

NOBOTS

ISBN 978-0-9910531-0-0

Printed in the United States of America

Table of Contents

Dedications:

To Patty, who said she liked it when it wasn't even half done

To Leila, who won't see this because she doesn't like to read

To Felbers, where part of it was written

To Slashdot, where the first draft was written, and to the slashdotters who commented and affected its content. It would be a different book and, I think, not nearly as good, without slashdotters' inputs. It might not have been written if not for slashdot.

To computers. I could not have written this using a pen or a typewriter. I wouldn't have been able to afford the warehouse full of paper, let alone the time to rewrite and correct.

Chapter 1

Little Green Men

Rority lounged back in his recliner, sipping his gargleblaster and puffing his stratodoober as the sun shone on his pale gray skin. Life was good.

He'd recently returned from a trip to prehistoric times, back even before firearms had been invented, let alone the discovery of atomic power. It was a good trip, because the ancient protohumans had documented his visit. Of course, the protohumans had couched it in religious terms; it was kind of strange that he, Rority, would be seen as an angel.

He grinned at the thought of a drunken, stoned angel. But because it had been documented in a book called "Ezekiel", he had to go back to make sure it had happened, or it wouldn't have. If *that* had happened, the timeline might have been distorted and the protohumans might have exterminated themselves, as the mathematicians had so carefully pointed out to him with numbers.

He was still trying to make a drink he'd discovered on the trip that the ancient protohumans called "beer". He'd tried it and found that the gargleblasters were weak, pale shadows of what the ancients had.

"Hey, Rority, how's that 'beer' stuff coming?"

Rority looked up – it was his good friend and partner, Gumal.

"Well," Rority said, "from the instructions it'll take another couple of days. I hope I got the formula right."

"Don't you mean 'recipe'?" Gumal twittered as another chair seemed to assemble itself from nothingness, the invisibly microscopic nobots arranging themselves to the reclining chair shape. “They didn't have science ten million years ago, you know.” He sat down on the nobotic reclining chair.

“Smartass. You know the difference between a chemist and a cook?”

“What?”

“The same difference between a physicist and a chemist!”

“That's the dumbest joke I ever heard,” Gumal snorted.

“What do you expect?” Rority said, snickering. “It's a ten million year old joke.”

“The joke's on you, pal,” replied Gumal. “They've got another trip planned for us.”

“Shit. When to now? Is it a dangerous mission?”

“The worst. It isn't anthropology or biology, we have to make sure the timeline stays intact.”

Rority sighed. “Damn. You don't want to tell me, so it must be pretty bad.”

“It is. We’re going to have to die, and be dissected.”

“God damn it!” Rority exclaimed. “I hate resurrection! It takes forever to get my memory right, and the dying itself is even worse. Shit!”

“But Rority, you know good and well if we don’t take this mission you'll never have existed, and neither will I have. The arithmetic boys say that if we don't go, the protohumans will have had some sort of catastrophe that destroyed them – and we're descended from them.

“And look at the brighter side – you don't have to have sex with a neanderthal.”

“You’re an asshole, asshole,” Rority said, grinning. “I didn't have sex with her, and she wasn't a neanderthal. She was a protohuman and it was the nobots that artificially inseminated her, you dickweed.”

Of course, they being from ten million years in the future and we being only protohumans who could understand our descendants even less than stone age men would be able to understand us, this is about as close as I can come to conveying what was actually said; our limited intelligence can't comprehend them at all.

There is no way could we understand their humor, and we might not even think it was funny even if we could understand it.

Needless to say, the humans could understand us perfectly well, and we could probably understand them about as well as a chimpanzee could understand us. But it's a rough approximation, nevertheless.

Gumal laughed. “Lighten up, dude! Where's your sense of humor? The funniest part was you having to go back and undo it, because it turned out that she had a parthenogenesis.” He laughed even harder.

Rority snickered. “OK, asshole. Let me read up on it.” Rority held his hand out, and a book appeared in it, again seemingly out of thin air, assembling itself out of the microscopic networked robots. Almost everything but food and drink was made out of nobots. A protohuman would have thought it magic, rather than technology.

Rority read the book, which was, of course, nothing like the books we protohumans have. Neither paper nor an electronic device, it appeared to be a single, thin sheet of cardboard which changed its text and illustrations with the movement of the reader's eyes.

“Wow, these protohumans are... did they really think we come from Mars?”

“Well, you have to remember,” Gumal pointed out, “that they'd not been to Mars or any other planet, not even to the moon. Not even their crude robots (if you could call their robots ‘robots’) had been there. They hadn't even been outside the Earth's atmosphere.”

“Yes but...” Rority said, “they knew about how diverse life is on Earth, but they expected extraterrestrials to look as much like them as they looked like simians? It's just absurd! Even after they got their primitive machines to Mars, they had fiction with space aliens looking more like themselves than we do.

“I can't comprehend how they couldn't understand that if you can go faster than light, you can travel through time as well. After all, the protohuman Einstein had figured out relativity and the Cosmic Constant twenty years or so before we'll be then.”

“Well, come on, they're only animals. Protohumans, not true humans. They were barely sentient.”

“I guess. Well, lets get going. And hey, look on the bright side – they have BEER. And it's even better beer than the beer we drank five thousand years earlier!”

Chapter 2

Martians

Private first class O'Brien lounged back in his recliner, sipping flavored water and munching on something salty and crunchy. The game was going well, with the New Salem Rorigars beating the snot out of the Norwegian Nebulans.

Watching sports got his mind off of his horribly nasty job. O'Brien hated his job.

Watching took his mind off of his floater, too. It had been operating erratically, and he might have to take it to a mechanic for adjustment or even repairs. It was surely going to be expensive.

It also kept his thoughts away from his wife's nagging him to throw his raggedy cobblobbers away. He liked his comfortable old cobblobbers and hated breaking in a new pair.

The O'Briens lived on Mars, which had been terraformed millions of years earlier. A hole had been dug all the way to its core, a giant molten magnet inserted, and most of the entire asteroid belt moved to the surface of the planet. An atmosphere similar to Earth's was generated chemically, with higher levels of carbon dioxide and oxygen and lower levels of nitrogen. Still not as massive as the Earth, its atmospheric pressure was three quarters of Earth's. Oceans were provided by comets and much of Saturn's rings.

It was no longer the red planet, even though people strangely still called it that. With its mostly nitrogen atmosphere, the Mars was almost as blue as the Earth.

The Martians had evolved to be tall, or at least tall compared to us protohumans. They had large chests and spindly legs, with smaller heads than Rority's or Gumal's. Their pale skin showed, predictably, their distance from the sun.

They would have all looked really, really weird to us protohumans. Laughably weird.

The early settlers who had colonized Mars millions of years earlier had it very rough, many of them dying at early ages. Even "terraformed" it wasn't exactly like Earth and was very inhospitable to the early immigrants. The environment was different enough that the Martians had evolved to better fit it.

Early Martian settlers had trouble growing crops in the lowered nitrogen atmosphere, but chemical fertilizers took up the slack. Later, of course, plants evolved and were bred to need less nitrogen.

Mars needed the carbon dioxide to keep it warm, especially since the removal of the asteroid belt had gravitationally shifted its orbit a tiny bit towards Jupiter.

Some Martians thought, in hindsight, that had they expended the energy necessary to pull the asteroids from the far side of the sun instead of the closest denizens of the belt, their orbit would have shifted towards the Earth's orbit rather than away from it, and they could have added more oxygen and nitrogen and less carbon dioxide.

It probably wouldn't have made any difference and certainly would not have been feasible, but hindsight is almost as mistaken as foresight sometimes. The ancient Martians had been smarter than the modern Martians gave them credit for, and had taken orbital shifting into account.

They had worried about the orbit moving closer to Earth, and worried about the two planets actually colliding. Something similar had happened billions of years earlier, when a planet the size of Mars had slammed into Earth and splashed, giving Earth more mass and giving it rings. The rings had gravitationally coalesced over time into the Earth's moon.

Nobody knew if the Martians could still breed with the people left behind on Earth. They assumed there had been evolution there, considering the Milankovitch cycles and the warming and cooling caused by them, but they didn't know.

It also wasn't known how the Amish wound up in charge of the Earth, outlawing most technology, or why the technorati had decided to leave and take their technology with them. History had been lost in the mists of time, especially since the early Martians had faced such hardships.

Even though doing research was their reason to move to Mars, once they were there they had little time for science and no time at all to record history. Just staying alive was a full time job.

But millions of years later, most modern Martians lived well, and study was Martians' passion.

O'Brien had just gotten home from work a while earlier and missed part of the game, which hadn't quite gotten his mind off of his disgusting job. He contemplated how it was ironic that Martians would have such a thing as sports, while the Venusians didn't.

"Venusians," O'Brien spat, in his mind. "Nasty, vulgar bastards, always after nothing but pleasure for themselves and pain and misery for everyone else." You would expect the Venusians to like the violently peaceful sports and the peaceful wars between sports teams.

The problem, he thought to himself, was the "peaceful" part. Venusians hated peace; they called it boredom. "Stupid Venusians," he thought, "always wanting to copulate or fight and do nothing else."

There was a tiny bit of ironic hypocrisy here, too, since O'Brien was in the Martian military and he and his wife had longed for a child.

Of course, Mars' military never did any fighting; their only purpose for existence was to be there in case the Venusians decided to stupidly attack them again, or even more unlikely, someone from another galaxy would attack, or a stray meteor from the Oort cloud might hit. The Martian military was prepared for any emergency, no matter how impossibly unlikely it was. Out of the billion Martians on Mars, only a few thousand were in the military. There were more sports players and entertainers than soldiers.

He decided to change his view of the game and adjusted a control. The holographic wall's scene swung around, with the strange, or would be to you anyway, sensation that the room itself was spinning. It would be strange to you unless, of course, you were drunk, in which case it would seem perfectly normal.

Fifty seven to forty seven. “Go, Rorigars!”

“Honey, dinner's on the table,” his wife said, walking in from the kitchen. “Hey, what are you doing eating those cow chips? I told you dinner was almost done!”

“Sorry, Precious, I was hungry. I still am. You mind if I watch the rest of the game in the dining room?”

Dennis smiled. She loved her husband, and was proud of his work, even though a life in the military wasn't held in high esteem on Mars by very many others. Martians loved learning; the only one more respected than a teacher was a researcher, and the only vocation held in less esteem than a soldier was a sports player. Even entertainers were more highly respected than a soldier, which was little at all.

“OK,” she answered, “but I want to watch the news. How much longer is the game going to be on?”

“It's almost ov... YEAH! Pointdown!” A buzzer's whistling screech sounded from the holographic display. “That was a good game, and honey, your timing was perfect! Lets eat! What are we having?”

“Cowburgers and shrimp fries, with mashed oglos and poopers.”

“Yum!” he said. His wife was a well known chef, and a very good one. O'Brien especially loved her poopers, and her cowburgers were hailed planet wide.

Back on the base, O'Brien's boss was uneasily looking at his screens and checking the electromagnetic radiation from Venus. No one knew any longer why the Venusians had originally left Earth, but the Martians suspected that the

Earthians those millions of years ago had used Venus as a penal colony, where their worst criminals were exiled.

"Shit," muttered Sargent Zales under his breath. "Damned Venusians. This doesn't look good at all. I'd better call Lieutenant Maris."

Chapter 3

Venusians

General Washington sat down on the beautiful golden throne that was ornately decorated with silver, platinum, and different precious gems, and frowned.

Washington's metal colored skin, which had evolved in the millions of years since Venus had been terraformed and populated to reflect the harsh Venusian sun's blazing light, gleamed brightly.

As he sat down, the sickly institutional green walls changed color to a royal purple. This technology had been obtained from a Martian defector during the last war a hundred years earlier.

The defector was probably the biggest reason the Martian military was so looked down on by the Martian populace; he had been the high ranking officer responsible for the deaths of the hundreds of Martians who had died in that war. He'd given orders to retreat when victory without loss had been assured. The deaths had all been civilians; not a single soldier was the least bit injured.

Angela Picard had been a cowardly traitor, and the wall coloring technology wasn't the only technical knowledge he'd passed to the enemy. Of course, strategic data and other important and dangerous intelligence was passed as well as technology, and the entire Martian army had taken the punishment. It was illogical and unfair, but that's just how it was.

The defector was a well known sports figure as well as being in the military, a basketball player. After the war, basketball's rules and its name were changed, because the sport itself was shunned afterward. Sports in general had lost their appeal and weren't really very popular any more.

Even our Martians descendents in the very far future aren't very logical.

Washington was holding his scepter in his right hand, with the bejeweled ornamental sword on his left leg shining more brightly than his strange skin, and his fully functional microwave pistol on the right. Five golden stars sat gleaming and sparkling on each of his shoulders, contrasting in color with his royal purple garments.

The General ruled an entire world. More, really - he *owned* an entire world. His edicts were law and he answered to no one. It was his to do with whatever he wished, titles be damned.

Right now he wished a lot of Venusians would commit suicide, or murder each other, and spare him the pleasure of killing them himself.

A semicircle of thirteen chairs, with twelve of them occupied by his highest officials, sat in front of him. The thirteenth chair sat empty to remind the officials of how easily they could be removed, and just what "removal" meant.

As if the crucified skeletons surrounding the palace weren't enough of a hint.

He spoke gravely. "Gentlemen, this planet is vastly overpopulated. Five billion is too many of us to sustain. People are going hungry, which isn't the problem. The problem is the unrest it's causing. We, the rulers of this planet, have it good and if it gets screwed up you'll wish you'd been castrated, burned, flogged, crucified, and eaten by the shambler. What do you suggest?"

General Ford, Secretary of War and Washington's second in command, spoke first. "Your eminence, I suggest we emigrate half the population. Earth is empty, nobody but a couple hundred thousand farmers with no weapons or technology at all. They're ripe for the picking!"

Secretary Zak interrupted. “Who would want to live there? A planet named after dirt? Disgusting place. I wouldn't even want to visit, let alone live there!”

“Yes, Ford,” said Washington, ignoring Zak. “But the Martians would never allow it. You know what happened the last time we tangled with those ugly little chalk-faced bastards, even though they're cowardly wimps and are nothing but nerdy little bookworms. Venus, but I hate those damned chalkies!”

“Well, sir, perhaps we could have a little warfare of our own?” asked Ford. “Say, an insurrection in a couple of provinces that we could put down with great loss of life?”

Washington smiled an evil grin. “I like it, Ford. Actually I'd like to kill all the damned chalkies, too, but the bastards are too damned sneaky and get us every time. The insurrection will only help a little bit, but it's better than nothing and will keep the populace's mind off their hunger. Mister Greenwalls, what does the Department of Justice suggest?”

“Well, sir, there aren't enough capital crimes. We're way too lenient. Make donating blood to family a capital offense. Give standing orders that any citizen who gets out of line and talks back to authority gets rayed instead of just having his tongue amputated.”

“I'll consider it, Mister Greenwalls. Zak, what does the Department of Commerce say?”

“Nothing, sir,” said Secretary Zak confidently. “We've already acted. An, ahem, ‘accident’ took down all the power generation in fifteen southern provinces. No power means no water, so most of them will be dead in a week.”

Washington stood, and the walls changed from the royal purple to a blood red.

“I see,” Washington said, circling behind his officials, who knew better than to look back at him. “Idiot! You could topple us all!”

“But, s-sir, it's, it's, uh, sir p-please,” he stammered before his head rolled across the floor, blood spraying everywhere from the obscenely flailing corpse it had been detached from.

"How about that?" said Washington, looking at his bloody sword and the hideous mess it had made. "It's not just for ceremony after all!"

Chapter 4

Farmers

They had farmed all their lives. Their parents, too, had farmed all their lives. They were farmers, had farmed forever, did what farmers did and lived like farmers lived. They grew crops and raised animals and were completely self-sufficient. There was nothing they needed or wanted that they couldn't grow or make for themselves.

They had been farmers for longer than anyone knew. They had long ago outlawed all but the most primitive of technologies; their holy text had forbidden them. The holy text was thought to have never changed, although it must have, since language itself changes.

The books were produced by a more than ancient method called woodcutting that was an allowed, primitive form of technology that had seemingly existed forever. The words were chiseled out of a wooden plank, inked with a roller, and pressed to paper.

All of their allowed technologies had existed since the beginnings of the Earth, according to their teachings.

Jonah drove the wagon through the light rain. "Sure was a great sermon John gave yesterday," he said.

"Yes, it was," Rebekkah agreed. "I especially liked the part about treating others like you'd like to be treated yourself.

"Did you hear the Jenkins were going to have a baby?" she said, changing the subject.

"No, I didn't. God has blessed them so?" Jonah said, startled. It's a great thing! Perhaps some day God will see fit to let us have a child."

His wife frowned. “Jonah!” she admonished. “Thou shalt not tempt the Lord thy God!”

“I'm not, honey. His will be done, not mine,” he whined. “But it would be nice if it was his will.”

The horse snorted.

Nobody knew or cared what the horse thought. Which was a pity, since its thoughts were very interesting.

Interesting to a horse, anyway. It wasn't paying the least bit of attention to Jonah and Rebekkah, being only mindful of the things horses care about, whatever it is that horses actually do care about.

The farmers used horses and mules to pull their plows and wagons, used candles and oil lamps for light, and lived simple lives. On the whole, they were happy. Their holy book spoke of a battle fought long ago between good and evil, and evil had been vanquished.

The rain was still lightly falling as the Muldoons' wagon pulled up to the barn. Joyful music was wafting out, its contemporary recreations of more than ancient musical instruments happily making a joyful sound and lightening one's heart, despite the rather inconvenient wetness.

“God's blessing us and our crops with his rain, Jonah,” said Rebekkah. “Not that we're short of it, but it's welcome anyway.”

“Yes, it is,” he answered, smiling.

The horse was happy, too. The rain meant that there weren't any flies.

The horse didn't like flies.

The Reverend Smith walked up as they entered the barn. “Good evening, John!” Muldoon said. “Beautiful night, isn't it?”

“Yes it is, Jonah. Well, except this rain, anyway. Come over here and have a glass of wine, you two.”

They clinked glasses. “To Yeshua!” said all three in unison. “Look at all that food!” exclaimed Rebekkah.

“We really did need this rain, though,” said Jonah. “It was dry while we planted that first field, praise the Lord!”

“Speaking of God's blessings, did you hear about the McDaniels boy?” Asked the preacher. “Fell down an empty well, must have been thirty or forty yards down.”

“Oh, my,” said Rebekkah. “Was he badly hurt? When did this happen?”

“This afternoon. He wasn't hurt at all! It was truly a miracle; Johnnie said it was dark and he couldn't see, but he could feel something gently catching him as he fell. His dad went down on a rope to get him, with four other men pulling them back up.”

“Truly a miracle,” Jonah agreed, smiling.

The instrumental tune that was playing as they spoke was, oddly, a tune you might recognize. The words that had gone with it were not only long forgotten but completely obsolete. The obsolete, long forgotten words to the tune that was playing wordlessly went:

Amazing grace, how sweet the sound that saves a wretch like me. I once was lost but now I'm found. Was blind, but now I see.

There were no longer wretches, no one was lost, no one was blind – everyone could see the good Lord's work clearly.

It might have applied to poor Johnny while he was in the dry well.

“Did you hear about the Jenkins?” Rebekkah asked.

“No,” said the preacher. “What about them?”

“They're going to have a baby! I'm surprised you didn't hear about it before anyone else.”

“No,” said the preacher, “it's news to me. Great news, praise the lord! Are they looking for a boy or a girl?”

“What does it matter?” said Jonah. “It's a rare blessing either way,” silently praying for God's blessing of the miracle of life to be bestowed on him and Rebekkah as well. Jonah envied the Jenkins, and had been remorseful of his covetous thoughts ever since his wife had scolded him while riding the buggy. Envy was a sinfully bad thing.

"Yes, Jonah, you're right," the preacher said. "I don't know of any blessing the good Lord could endow on one that would be a greater blessing, praise his name! Where did you hear it from, Rebekkah?"

"Sarai told me herself when I held communion with her this morning. I've never seen anybody as happy as her!"

After the dance, when the Muldoons were back at home and in post-coital bliss, again Rebekkah said "How I love God!"

Of course, she was a little jealous of the Jenkins, too. Just a little, but she would never admit it to anyone.

What a lucky couple the Jenkins were!

Chapter 5

The Death of Two Protohumans

"I'm not going!"

"Yes you are. You have to."

"No I don't. You know the law." Rority was correct; he was perfectly within his rights. There was only one law – do what you want, or do nothing if that's what you wish. Unlike the poor protohumans millions of years previously, nobody had to work. In fact, there was nothing the protohumans would have called "work," anyway. The protohumans would have called what these folks called "work" a hobby. The nobots provided all the food, shelter, clothing, entertainment, everything a person could ever want.

With the planet's population fixed at two million people after the Great Catastrophe several millions of years earlier had almost wiped them out and had caused the largest mass extinction in the planet's life, there was plenty of land for everyone. Want your street paved with gold? The nobots would pave your street with gold if that's what you wanted, molecule by molecule. There were enough nobots to do it quickly.

The law would have seemed strange to us, their uber-ancient ancestors. Do anything you want? Steal? Kill? Rape? Cheat? Swindle?

But theft itself was obsolete; the uncounted numbers of nobots, the microscopic machines that had at first been called nano-robots, which was shortened to "nanobots", then "nobots" after nanoscale was large in comparison to the size of the microscopic nobots, made property a quaint anachronism.

Each microscopic nobot contained more computational processing power than the biggest computer the protohumans had ever built, and could sample mechanical vibrations or electromagnetic radiation, and produce the same, as well as manipulate individual molecules, atoms and subatomic particles.

Anything one wanted one only had to ask for, and it would be assembled instantly by the nobots. Want a few billion trillion more nobots? The nobots would get the raw materials and construct them.

Murder? There was no longer any motive for murder, even if murder was possible. The nobots made injury or death an impossibility. They would assemble themselves into armor that would stop any weapon one could dream up, and if the impossible had ever become possible, pain had been genetically engineered out of people. Should someone, for instance, fall off a cliff and and the impossible happened that he had actually hit bottom, the nobots would be in his body already, performing microscopic surgery on every injured cell.

Rape? Unthinkable. The nobots could assemble themselves into a simulacrum of the object of desire, only more desirable, and besides, rape is a crime of violence and hate rather than passion. There was no longer any reason for hate, even if hatred hadn't been genetically engineered out of them like pain had. In fact, hatred and pain were connected in the same genes that had been removed. Without pain there can be no hatred.

Cheat? Swindle? Cheat and swindle out of what?

Gumal frowned; even this was unusual. "But Rority, if you don't go I'll have to!"

"No you won't."

"But somebody has to!"

"Why?"

"You read the report, didn't you?"

"Yes," said Rority. "That's why I don't want to go."

"But look," argued Gumal, "this one's easy."

"Sorry, Gumal, I'm not going. I told you before."

"But look," Gumal repeated, "you don't mind the genetic reprogramming and changing of your form to match the protohumans, you said so yourself. You told me you even *liked* some of the protohumans."

"That's one reason I'm not going," Rority said. "I particularly like the one I'd have to kill..." He shuddered again at the word, "and damn it, I know what a broken leg feels like and I'll have to get my leg broken. I don't want to know what it feels like to be shot inside a burning barn!"

"You don't have to. Look, all you have to do is shoot the guy, throw the other guy off of the balcony, and get back to your ship.

"No! I have an appreciation for this particular animal. I met him before, when he was a lawyer in Springfield. I learned a lot of protohistory from studying him and I don't want to shoot him. I'm just not going to do it."

"OK," Gumal sighed, "I'll shoot the crazy bastard myself. How about shooting this one? It's about a hundred years later."

"That's another reason I don't want to do it. All the similarities are just too weird; you know how time works, with its impossible paradoxes if something goes wrong, and I suspect something went wrong with the timeline just because of the odd coincidences. You know that whatever I'm going to do was already done, looking at things from a future perspective."

"OK, damn it, I'll shoot him, too. How about this assignment? I just got it from Rula. Here." Gumal handed Rority the nobotic book and Rority read it over.

"Hey, now this one I like! Going back to the first time traveler and making sure nobody ever travels farther into the future than he already has been. Yep, I do like this one. It's like this protohuman fiction I just finished reading," he said, holding a small sheaf of real paper wrapped on three sides in real cardboard.

"You and your primitive books!" Gumal snorted.

"Want a hit?" Rority asked.

"Sure thing," Gumal said, taking a toke from Rority's stratodoober. "By the way, what *is* that protohuman book you just finished reading?"

"It actually has to do with the reason for the assignment I just accepted. It's in a genre called 'science fiction' even though most of the books and especially videos of this genre have very little science, sometimes none at all, and they often get the science wrong when there's any science at all in them.

"*The End of Eternity* is the name of this book, it's one of the better ones. It was written by a protohuman biochemist and cancer researcher named Isaac Asimov. He wrote it some time in the first part of the first century.

"Tripe!" Gumal exclaimed.

"Pretty damned good for a barely sentient animal," Rority replied.

Chapter 6

Ghouls

"Hey, Larry, can you help me with this?"

"Sure, George," O'Brien said. "What's the problem?"

"I can't hear Washington," said Private Williams. Williams was new, only out of basic training a few days earlier.

"Let's see," said O'Brien. "Hmmm... looks like none of the 'scopes can see his lips, so of course you can't hear him. Just listen to what the guy he's talking to is saying and sometimes you can figure out what Washington's saying, too. How's your Venusian?"

"Not that good yet, Larry. I haven't had much practice at this."

"Well, just watch the translation crawl at the bottom of the screen. In a couple of weeks you'll be talking ghoulish like you were born on Venus."

"Ghoulish? I don't get it."

"Watch the screens long enough and you will. I hope you don't have a weak stomach, George, because those Venusians are some damned nasty bastards."

"Well hey, Larry, I wouldn't have volunteered for Venuswatch if I couldn't stand a little blood."

O'Brien laughed. "You're going to see a lot worse than a little blood. Ever seen a man strangled by his own intestines? Ever see anybody skinned alive and sodomized with his own dick?"

Williams looked a little queasy. "That bad?"

"Worse," said O'Brien. "It won't be long before you find out what those plastic bags are for."

"What *are* they for?"

“They're vomit bags. I don't care how strong your stomach is, you're going to be puking. Those Venusians are just downright nasty. Just be glad the telescopes don't deliver smells as well as sight and voice, I hear they smell as bad or even worse than the nasty ghouls look and act.”

“Damn, I had no idea. Why didn't they tell us?”

“They tried. Hey, any time you want to transfer or resign, well, that's your right. I gotta tell you, though, that even though the Sarge is a gunghole, he's right. The Venusians have attacked us before and they'll attack us again. The sons of bitches just can't keep their pants on, don't believe in birth control, are dumber than boxes of rocks and meaner than a rabid werewharg in heat.”

Meanwhile, the screen wasn't telling them much. Washington was in a rocket facility talking to an underling, and all that could be heard was the underling.

O'Brien absentmindedly wondered why the satellites' telescopes couldn't pick up sound. If the resolution was high enough, they should be able to measure vibrations on surfaces and reconstruct the waveforms and play them back through the speakers.

Maybe he'd talk to Lieutenant Maris about it. Someone smarter than him could surely figure out how to come up with the technology.

The underling on the screen said “Yes sir. No sir. Uh, where, sir? I see, sir, may I ask why? Of course, sir, need to know. I understand, sir. Yes sir, we'll get right on it. I'd say we can lift off immediately, General.”

Washington walked out of the facility, and O'Brien wished he could have heard him. “Well, George, what do you think?” O'Brien asked Williams.

“I think those are some damned ugly, evil looking sons of bitches,” Williams replied. “They do look like ghouls! They sound like ghouls, too.”

O'Brien laughed. “Yeah, they are, but what do you think of the conversation, even if you could only hear one side?”

"Not much, sorry."

"You'll get the hang of it. Washington's up to something, and the only something he's ever up to is no good. It looks like he's going to launch a few rockets and maybe try to take out the satellites we have around Venus. He must suspect that some of his men are traitors or he'd be less secretive; he didn't say anything about this to his council of ministers. That's only a guess, based on what we've seen before. But who knows, he might be planning an attack on Earth or Mars."

"Why Earth?" asked Williams. "They're no threat to Venus."

"Neither are we, and we never have been, but they attack us every time they get enough technology to reach us, anyway. They're just evil, bad evil, the worst. Evil isn't even a strong enough word for their brand of evil.

"They're overpopulated and want to run the entire solar system, and they don't want anybody but Venusians to live, and they don't even care much about their fellow Venusians either, just themselves. They've evolved to love killing.

"Earth is mostly empty of people, only a few hundred thousand farmers and no technology at all," O'Brien continued. "Hell, the protohumans we were both descended from had more technology. The Earthians don't even use electricity, they'd be a pushover if it weren't for us. If the Venusians ever took Earth, Mars would be a hell of a lot easier to conquer too, so yes, we're doing it out of charity but we're protecting our own interests at the same time."

Williams said "Hey, we can hear Washington now, but he's only giving directions to his driver. They're going to another rocket facility."

"Well, hell," said O'Brien. "Another one? Maris should hear about this. Watch those screens close, now, and if you need help just yell. I'll be right around the corner working on a report when I get done talking to the Lieutenant."

“Wait a minute, Larry, what's this ‘hark’ shit?”

“Nothing, George, just some Venusian stupidity. When one of their superiors shows up they say ‘hark’. Sounds like they have a cough or something, don't it?”

Williams laughed. “Yeah, it does. Man, I feel like I'll never understand these guys.”

“Don't feel bad, you'd have to be crazy to understand what motivates those fuckheads.”

Williams laughed again. “Fuckheads? I never heard that one, either!”

“Yeah,” said O'Brien, “Fuckheads. All they think about is fucking, and when there's nothing to fuck they fight. Watch those screens!”

“Shit, Larry, they're launching!” Williams said, panicking like green Martian recruits always did at the first hint that Venus was going to be rude again.

“Where are they on the countdown?” O'Brien asked.

“Thirty minutes.”

“I'll get Maris. Damn.”

“Come in,” Maris said, answering O'Brien's knock.

“Sir, the Venusians are launching a rocket,” O'Brien said.

“Manned?”

“Yes, sir.”

“How many crew?”

“Unknown, sir. And it's a huge ship.”

“Well, I don't think we need to worry about them yet, Private. If they're trying to take out the self-defending satellites we have there they're fried meat. If they're heading here, EL2 will take them out. Maybe it's innocent.”

“Innocent? Sir? They're Venusians!”

“Yes, it certainly would be unusual for them. I wonder where that thing could be going? I'm curious. There's no hurry to shoot.

“Thank you, Private. Dismissed.”

Chapter 7

Stratodoober Madness

"Ugh! Damn, Son of a bitch! This is really nasty! This shit really tastes like shit!" Gumal swore in disgust. "This isn't the same beer you brought back from ancient Englarsh, or whatever the name of that damned place was."

He took a toke off the stratodoober to clear the nasty taste out of his mouth and, more to the point, forget he'd ever tasted it.

"Huh?" Rority replied, "It isn't. These are some different brands from some different breweries. It's called Moosehead. It's from Carnudia, Carnivore, Cannalida, something like that. I forgot what they called the damned place. I haven't tried it. Here, I'll trade you, this one's from Germie Man."

He took a sip of the Moosehead. "Ugh! Gimme that stratodoober!"

"I have trouble reading these protohuman scribblings," Gumal said. "What is it?"

"Heiney Kin. I have no idea why they gave beers these silly names, related to a gluteus maximus?

"Hey, I got a great idea. Noboty, come here."

"Yes, sir?" replied the robot, constructed from trillions of nobots, of course.

"I want an Irish pub. No, wait - not a real pub like in real ancient Ireland, but something better. That place we were that time in Springfield when we stopped for a few cases of beer fifty years or so after Gumal killed Kennedy. Lets see, what was it called? Dancies? Dracies'?"

"D'Arcy's Pint, sir?" the nobotic butler inquired respectfully. "Rather primitive, isn't it, sir?"

"Well sure, of course. That's the whole point. But if you want primitive, go back only a hundred thousand years earlier than then."

"That's not in my data banks, sir, but I could interface." The robot "thought" for a second, then replied "which D'Arcy's, sir?"

Gumal interrupted. "This tastes almost as bad as the Moosehead. When did you get this gawdoffal swill?"

"Three trips ago, maybe a few months."

Gumal had been researching the ancient art... no, far more than ancient, since the art of brewing beer had died out millions of years before. Rority had tried his hand at making his own and failed miserably, even though he was as far advanced in intelligence to a protohuman as a protohuman was as far advanced in intelligence as an Australopithecus. It would be twice that, if humans hadn't stopped evolving five million years earlier.

It kind of galled him that a barely sentient animal could out think him in basic chemistry, especially since chemistry as such no longer existed; it was pure physics now.

Maybe that was the problem, he thought.

"Well, there's your answer, Gumal pontificated. "It got skunky."

"What? What's 'skunky' mean"?

"You know that one animal, the black one with the white stripe down its back? Well, before we reconstituted all the extinct species and made the dangerous ones harmless and limited animals' breeding abilities, this particular one defended itself with a nasty stench from a gland under its tail. It was called a 'skunk'. The protohumans said that beer got 'skunky', meaning bad tasting and bad smelling."

"Shit. Then all my beer's bad?"

"How old is it?"

"Ten million years, protobrain!"

Gumal laughed. “No, I mean how long since you brought it to the present?”

“I already told you, the newest is at least a few months old.”

“Did you keep it cold?” asked Gumal

“Only the Ameran Corn stuff,” Rority explained. “They drank it cold, everybody else drank theirs at room temperature.”

“OK”, said Gumal, “What kind of Ameriwhatever beer do you have?”

“Well, there's Busch, Bud...”

“They named the beer plants' names?” Gumal interrupted again. “Makes more sense than butt relatives from Germie Man, I guess. After all, they did make it out of barley and hops and other grains. But the grains didn't come from bush buds, they came from grasses.”

“Who knows why a protohuman would name their stuff the silly names they gave it?” Rority said “Anyway, there's Cores, and Milner, and San Paulie, and Carumba, and dufus' exes... hey, I bet they named that one after the dumb brewmaster's wives!”

He thought a second. “No, those two were only refrigerated in the northern part of the Hundred States; it was before the continent became one country.”

“Are you sure?”

“No,” Rority replied, “I didn't do any extensive research or anything. Hey, robot, how's that pub coming?”

“You never did say which one, sir.”

“Oh... there was more than one? The one I was in.”

“That would be the one they built after they lost their lease in the strip mall,” the robot replied.

“The what?” Gumal asked. “They took their clothes off and mauled each other?”

“No, sir,” the robot answered. “A ‘mall’ was an alley if I'm not mistaken,” like it ever would be, “and it was laid out in a strip. Strip mall.”

Rority said "Oh, hell, just make the whole damned town. How many people were in it?"

"Quite a few more than a hundred thousand people in the time period D'Arcy's Pint existed, sir."

"Well, you don't have to recreate the whole town. Just the pub and a kilometer or three surrounding it, and enough people to make it convincing."

"Yes sir."

Gumal said "open" and the bottle cap popped off. He took a sip of his Budweiser and made a face. "Almost drinkable. Better than a gargleblaster, anyway. It doesn't taste anything like a Guinness, though."

"Of course not," Rority said. "Guinness is a lager, Budweiser is a pilsner."

"What are lagers and pilsners?"

"Different beer recipes," Rority answered. "I thought you said you were researching it?"

Gumal looked at the label. "This says Budweiser was a lager. I'm not researching how they made it, you're doing that. Hey, what did they use to smoke hemp buds from back then? Maybe they were better at that than us, too."

Rority said "well, there were a few ways. There were pipes, bongs, hitters, doobies..."

"Is that anything like a stratodoober?"

"No, it was just a thin piece of paper with the plant material rolled up in it. You set one end on fire and inhale the smoke from the other end. The closest a protohuman could come to stratodoobing would be to burn a fattie while sitting on top of a mountain. Here, hey Noboty, roll Gumal a joint."

"Yes, sir," the robot said. It rolled a large joint, lit it with the end of its burning index finger, and handed it to Gumal.

"Burn a fattie?" Gumal asked, holding the burning fattie.

Rority laughed. "Set fire to a big fat doob. Like what's in your hand."

The joint went out out before Gumal took a toke, so he lit it again with a small nobotic device that looked a little like the cigarette lighters they used to install in automobiles before smoking was seen as a really, really bad thing.

"Hmmm..." Gumal said, after inhaling the sweet smoke deeply, and holding it a few seconds before letting it out. "Not too bad. Nowhere near as good as a stratodoober, but it will do."

"Your program is ready, sirs," the robot said. "Here's a doorway." It promptly dissolved into a waft of nobotic dust, and what would have looked like a very nice outhouse to your great great grandfather stood in its place.

Rority said "Hey, I wonder if Rula would want to come? She likes eating almost as much as she loves stratodoobing."

"Dunno, hey Rula!" Gumal said.

Rula's shape assembled itself out of nobots. "Yeah, guys, what's up?"

"Want to come to an old Amerin corn recreation of an ancient Irish pub?" Rority asked.

"No, thanks, I'm learning to dance. You know, Rority, your fascination with the protohumans is catching on."

"What's 'dance'?" Gumal asked.

"It's a protohuman thing, I'll show you some time. It's fun. Gotta go, though." She dissolved; or rather, her nobotic image dissolved into nobotic dust, and disappeared.

Gumal and Rority went into the very nice, if small, outhouse, which once inside past the large entrance area was a very nice and very big room that was very full of nobotic simulations of protohumans. There was a long bar, many tables, and there were ancient Irish musical instruments hanging from walls among posters that were advertising Guinness beer. There were video screens, and Rority noted again that they interestingly showed only two dimensional images rather than holograms.

“How many, sir?” the nobotic simulation of a hostess asked in the large entrance area, apparently unaware that Rority and Gumal looked less like protohumans than bonobos did.

“Two, please.”

“There's a two hour wait...”

“Pause nobots” Rority said. “No waiting. Make it not so busy. Continue.” Rority had forgotten how popular this place had been.

“Right his way,” the nobotic hostess said. “What would you like to drink?”

“I'll have a Guinness,” Rority said.

The hostess looked both woeful and exasperated. “Sorry, guys, but the beer distributors' drivers union is on strike. All we have is soft drinks. We're really sorry, we pride ourselves on our beer selection. There may be a case or two of Millers left.”

“Pause nobots,” Rority said. “Console.” He picked up a menu and spoke into it. “Real reason for no beer?” The console read

Error code #476,480,937,821: Limited supplies available

Requested item only available from past

Suggested substitute: Root Beer

Rority sighed. “Continue program,” he said, as the menu became a menu again.

When the drinks came, Rority thought that it was too bad there wasn't any real Guinness. He'd have to study this “draft beer” thing and incorporate it into the D'Arcy's program, as well as stocking it with a case of each of the other brands D'Arcy's had carried.

He hoped he didn't have the same problem with the food, which would be synthesized by nobots and probably wouldn't taste exactly like what he had eaten in the real place.

Rather than the blessing of Ireland's best, there was a sweet, dark, carbonated water drink the menu said was called root beer that the console had suggested.

Drinking it, Rority thought of another protohuman book he'd read that was written by one of the fellows the Irishmen who had invented Guinness had wanted to kill in terrible ways.

“This stuff tastes almost, but not quite, entirely unlike Guinness,” he said. “Here's to protohuman fiction!” he exclaimed, raising his glass.

Gumal made a face. “Tripe!” he said.

Rority snickered. “You didn't even read it!”

“I don't have to. You just quoted it. Jees, he was just an animal. Protohuman fiction is a quaint novelty, nothing more.”

“You underestimate them,” Rority said. “They were surprisingly clever sometimes. They did invent beer, you know, and we can't recreate it.”

He asked the artificial nobotic waitress if it was OK to smoke; he'd seen that there was some sort of law against smoking indoors. Not unreasonable, considering the primitive premedical protohuman society with its lack of nobotic cellular surgery, and all the other advancements and discoveries that had happened in the last ten million years.

“No sir,” she said, “but you can smoke outside on the patio.”

The two went outside and sat at a table next to a table that had an armed man dressed in a black costume with a shiny metal thing on his chest sitting at it.

Gumal relit the perfectly machine rolled joint the nobotic robot had made for him earlier.

“What the... Hey, you two! You're under arrest!” the armed and strangely costumed man said.

“What? PAUSE! End simulation! Son of a BITCH!” Gumal said. “Now you see why I hate those trips. Goddamned primitive!”

“Not as bad as the real thing was,” Rority replied. “I wonder why he was going to arrest us? I'm going to have to do a little research.”

“Who knows what the protobrain thought? Anyway, give me that stratodoober!” Gumal said as the pub and its contents dissolved around them.

Rula was leaning back on a recliner, sipping a gargleblaster.

“That ‘dancing’ stuff is exhausting,” she said. “Fun, but exhausting. I don't know how those protohumans could live like that. Got a beer, Rority?”

Chapter 8

Spies

General Ford's lips trembled slightly as he stood at attention. "I've failed, sir," he said. "I await execution. My life is in your hands, as my service has been by your grace."

"Nonsense," answered Washington. "The rebellion in the south cost over a million and a half lives, easing the population problem at least a little, while doing nothing to us except make us look good. And I've come up with the perfect plan for taking care of the Martians, the Earthians, and..." he chuckled, "those southern assholes. Notice how it's always the southerners who cause trouble? We're going to lose a lot of southerners, and it's going to look like it's the Martians' fault."

"But sir," said Ford, "may I ask how that's in any way possible, considering how much more technologically advanced they are?"

"No, Ford, you may not. There are Martian spies about, I'm sure of it, although I haven't been able to figure out how they're planting bugs. They've obviously actually been inside the palace itself.

"This is strictly on a need to know basis, and I don't want to put you in jeopardy. You're far too valuable.

"Dismissed, Ford."

"Yes Sir" said Ford, saluting.

Zales and O'Brien were watching from millions of kilometers away. "What do you make of that, Sarge?" asked O'Brien.

"Dunno, but it's especially worrisome considering all the rockets they launched today. It's also worrying that they've started to suspect that we can see and hear them. It's good, though," the Sargent said, "that they think we have spies actually on their planet and don't even suspect that we can see them on these screens, from all the satellites that we have orbiting Venus as well as the telescopes we have aimed at them from here and from the various Earthian La Grange points.

"Of course they can shoot a few satellites down once in a while, but our tech just moves too fast for them to do much damage to the umbrella. They're still using chemical rockets, for Galaxy's sake!

"It's a good thing they have such small imaginations, or they'd realize that the way we hear them is by having computers read their lips, and we can see right through their walls!"

"How far have the rockets gone? Are we going to shoot them down?" O'Brien asked.

"Lieutenant Maris says no, damn it. He says they may not be heading for Mars. In fact, he says they may be heading away from Mars, using the sun as a gravitational slingshot. That's what Maris says, anyway. Me, I think they're all just stupid and did the math wrong and they'll wind up smashing into the sun. I want to see that!

"The Lieutenant has sent a message to the Titanians, who will probably ignore it like they always ignore us. Maris says he can't figure out why they'd be sending rockets to Saturn unless they're planning on attacking the Titanians, but that would be senseless. Venusians can't live on Titan!"

"Hey, check this out, Sarge," O'Brien said, "Ford seems to be just aimlessly walking down the street."

"OK, Johnson, you watch Ford. O'Brien, keep track of Washington. The rest of the team needs to be watching, too. I don't like the looks of things."

"Shit, those guys are just plain evil! Look at this!" Johnson said as Ford decapitated a bystander.

"I can't, I'm too busy watching Washington."

Johnson watched Ford saunter down the street whistling, the ever present ugly, evil look on his face.

To a protohuman, a human Amish would look goofy, almost clown-like with their funny noses and ridiculously wide mouths. Martians would look even goofier, with their skinny legs and strange chests and large heads and comically weird faces. But one look at a Venusian would make your blood run cold. They *looked* evil. And they were.

As the second most powerful man on Venus walked along, passers by would salute and yell "Hark!"

Ford put a coker in a pipe and inhaled deeply, smiled an evil shit-eating grin, and laughed a chillingly evil laugh.

Cokers were processed from what was thought to be a native Venusian plant that had slight stimulant properties when chewed, but strong effects when processed and smoked. The plant was thought to be native to Venus, because it only existed on that planet. Of course, all life in the Milky Way started on Earth; life is an incredibly rare thing that appears in few galaxies.

Cokers combusted on inhalation. Ford burned another rock, and glowered. Cokers made Venusians more Venusian than Venusian. Ford loved his cokers.

And as Venus' second in command, he could have as much as he wanted of anything he wanted. Including coke rocks.

He burned yet another. His evil grin became even more evil looking as he stepped into the Dick and Pussy Saloon.

A group of teenagers was fist fighting in the corner, and Ford microwaved them, grinning as they burst into flames. The teenagers ran out of the door screaming "Hark! Hark!" at the top of their lungs before collapsing in the street, still on fire.

"Hark!" Yelled the bartender, snapping to attention. "Hark!" all the patrons echoed, also snapping to attention.

"At ease, boys, I just came for a little pleasure. Barkeep, give me a bloody Martian." he laughed an evil laugh. "In fact, kill all those damned wimpy Martian nerds and I'll have a *real* drink made out of real Martian blood! My grandpa says that those chalkies are really tasty, especially their blood."

The bartender laughed nervously. “Yes sir,” he gibbered.

“What the bullet are you laughing at, idiot? Are you laughing at ME?!”

“N-no, sir, of course not sir!”

Ford drew a weapon, pointed it, and the bartender's head exploded. “Well, you should have, moron, that was a joke! You,” he said, pointing at a patron. “You're the new bartender.”

“B-but sir,” he stuttered, “I don't know how to tend bar!”

His head exploded as well. “Anybody else in here that's not a bartender?” Ford said, sipping the drink the now-late bartender had concocted.

He looked around at the crowd. A group of wet-eared kids stupidly laughing, a couple in what was obviously the beginnings of a romantic interlude at a table, and... hey, he thought, she's damned good looking. Not to us, of course, but to a Venusian...

Ford sat down at their table. “Hey, beautiful, how about we get nekkid and fuck?”

The man's skin became as pale as aluminum and the woman's face blushed a copper color; a Venusian's metallic-looking skin's colors changed with his or her mood. “This man is my husband!” she objected.

Ford laughed an evil laugh. “Not any more,” he said as the man's head exploded and the woman screamed.

Ford holstered his pistol and said “You know, up close you don't look so good. Keep your clothes on, bitch.” As he walked through the exit, he said loudly “Drinks are on the dead bartender. I'm getting out of this boring fucking place, losers.”

As he exited the bar he ignored the children who were eating the corpses of the bunch he'd set on fire earlier.

A very attractive (to a Venusian, anyway) woman followed him. “General?” she said, “That bitch was stupid, I'd love to get naked and fuck!"

"Slut!" Ford exclaimed, as her bloody, headless corpse hit the sidewalk and laid there quietly with blood spewing out of its neck and urine running down its leg.

He didn't just want sex, he wanted foreplay - which included, of course, killing her already established man. If she had no man, why would the second most powerful Venusian on the planet want her?

"Hark, beautiful one!" a woman yelled. Ford turned. Not bad, he thought. Her man looked formidable, too. This might be fun.

"Get lost, loser," Ford said as he drew his gun, which went off at the same time as his opponent's weapon discharged. Ford's unfortunate opponent's chest exploded and he fell to the ground, blood spraying everywhere from the gaping hole in his corpse, as his bullet ricocheted from Ford's carbon fiber suit.

"Ow!" Said Ford. "Your man shot me! That was hot!"

"Oh, Venus' penis!" she exclaimed. "Oh, your worship, what can I do?"

"You can die, bitch," he said before her head exploded and her corpse hit the ground, blood spewing from its neck and its body flailing and twitching on the ground.

Sadly, all this was all perfectly normal behavior for a Venusian. Private Johnson was on Mars, and he and O'Brien had to watch this horror show.

"I need to look for a new job," Johnson said to himself. "This sucks. I hate it!"

Such was the life of a Martian military man. He had to watch this disgusting horror, but at least he didn't have to be there. Galaxy, would this shift never end?

Chapter 9

It's the End of the World (but I feel fine)

Gumal landed on the asteroid, planted the cloak, and pushed – just slightly. Just enough so it would make one more transit around the "big star", the Earth's star, before the gigantic thing smacked into the Earth.

By the ancient calendar it would strike in 347 AB; three hundred forty seven years after the first nuclear explosion on the Earth's surface.

The protohumans had seemed hell-bent on destroying themselves. In 20 AB, give or take a few years, they had nearly had an atomic apocalypse that they'd called the "Bay of Pigs Invasion", and then again in 40 or 50 AB when the heads of two superpowers sat in their respective offices across the globe, both drunk, and both ready to unleash atomic hell on each other. The dates were uncertain; the time was ten million years in the past.

Now they were flirting with disaster again, with East Pakindia and West Pakindia at each other's throats. At one time the two rivals had merged into a single country, but a civil war which was thankfully non-nuclear had split the two into separate nations again.

Both had atomic weapons.

Gumal was bringing real apocalypse. The Hindus and Buddhists called him "Shiva." The Christians, Jews, and Muslims called him "Gabriel".

His good friend and partner Rority called him "Asshole".

Rority was in his own ship, having undergone the nobotic genetic manipulations that made him almost a protohuman. He called Gumal on his timeceiver. "Did you move that rock, Gumal?"

"Yep. Are you in position?"

"Both space and time, asshole. You should be ashamed of yourself, killing all those helpless animals."

"You know good and damned well this has to happen or even viruses will be extinct. Yeah, I don't like doing it, but it has to be done."

Gumal was a little annoyed at Rority's jab. He knew full well what would happen if the rock didn't land, but he knew that Rority wasn't fully sentient right then, a hundred years future from Gumal's present, ten million years earlier than when they'd lived.

But it still annoyed him. He didn't want to do this, but it had to be done. Like he'd told Rority.

Ten minutes after the conversation, from Rority's perspective, the rock swooped past the sun and straight toward the Earth. They never saw it coming, thanks to the cloak, even though they had been watching for something like it for over three hundred years.

The cloak was a sheath of nobots that absorbed light and other electromagnetic waves on one side, then re-transmitted the signals to the opposite side, rendering it completely invisible to any electromagnetic wavelength. It shut down as it passed the sun, reassembled into a whole, and continued in a more or less parallel path with the gigantic mountain flying towards the Earth.

When they finally saw it, they freaked out, of course. Protohumans are panicky animals.

President Rodriguez of the Hundred States of America screamed at the governor of Chihuahua. "God damn it, your state's in charge of the space program. Now launch something to deflect that asteroid, or blow it up, or *something!*"

Like the conversations between Gumal and Rority, this, too is a translation, an approximation, as language had changed so much in three hundred years that we in the 21st century (by our quaint calendar) might catch a little of the meaning, if we were fluent in English, Spanish, Japanese, Mandarin, Arabic, Hindi; all six languages, plus parts and pieces of a few more languages that had morphed into the language that was spoken world wide by then.

Governor McDaniel sighed. Rodriguez was a moron, he thought to himself. How can I explain to this stupid idiot that the damned rock was just too big and too close to deflect? But he knew it wouldn't matter – they were all doomed.

"Sir," he said, "it's useless. It's too close, there's absolutely nothing we can do! We have to get off the planet!"

Ten billion people and countless animals were going to die, and the only ones that had a chance of survival were the very rich and powerful on their way off of the planet, and the parasites that lived off of these parasites.

Jim heard the horn blow; at least, it sure sounded like a horn. An incredibly big horn.

The sound was actually the asteroid whistling through the Earth's atmosphere. He got on his knees and prayed. "Our father in heaven, hallowed be thy name, please God forgive me my si..."

BOOOOOOOOOOOOOOOOOOOOOOOOOOM! The earth shook; even the Japanese had never experienced such a quake. He finished his prayer and headed to church; he knew what day it was.

Judgment day. Jesus was coming, and he was going to be taken to heaven. At least, he hoped and prayed he would; nobody sane wants to die, or worse, go to hell. He couldn't know that the only two fates for anybody were death, or hell. The ones who survived would live in hell, only the hell would be on Earth.

The flames rained from the sky later that day.

Gumal felt sick. Those poor, barely sentient protohumans. And the other animals as well – they had feelings, too. He wished he'd never let himself be transformed into one of them. He hated pain, even though he really couldn't understand it as a human, pain having been engineered out of humans millions of years earlier. But after you were a protohuman, you remembered. Sort of. Like a protohuman having come down from an LSD trip remembered the trip. Sort of. The brain wasn't the same.

Rority felt a great sadness; he liked protohumans. Some were like his pets, and he loved that protohuman beer. "Rority, are you receiving?" his timeceiver squawked.

"Yeah, Gumal, warping to four years from now in a minute or two. You OK? You don't sound OK."

"I'm not, Rority. I feel really bad – all those poor animals dead, and in pain." Gumal had been transformed into a pseudo-protohuman only a few times, and refused to do it again except for the most serious of circumstances, like when it was necessary because he wouldn't have been born if he didn't.

"They have feelings," he said, "and the protohumans are almost sentient."

"Yeah," said Rority, "they were smart enough to invent nuclear bombs and stupid enough to invent nuclear bombs. But look, dude, the ones who don't survive are going to live, and the ones who survive are not only going to die, but are going to be dead forever, with no chance of ever being resurrected."

"But only a few billion that were alive will be unaffected by the Grabonic radiation, which only affects certain types of people, and most of them will be sterile. No chance for the rest of them, they're dead forever."

"They didn't deserve a chance. You did your job well, Gabriel."

"Don't call me that, you son of a bitch!"

"Sorry, Gumal. Bad joke. Look, I'm warping, so you'll have to change freqordinates to pick me up. But dude, cheer up. It's a *good* thing you did."

Rority, having made sure the asteroid had hit the right spot on Earth, prepared for his trip forward.

Ten minutes later for Rority and four years later for the survivors of the catastrophe, President Rodriguez and Governor McDaniel and the rest of the United World council, as well as the glitterati and corporati and the other monied people who had survived the apocalypse were meeting in Jiplon; a town that had formerly been known as Joplin.

"This meeting will come to order," Secretary M'bago thundered.

"We're dying," he announced. "We, a few cats and dogs and rodents and some insects are all that survived," he said, "and we won't live much longer. I hereby..."

A robed man with brown eyes, a prominent nose, long black hair, and a beard shimmered into view facing him. Their jaws all dropped. "Wha... where... how... who are you?" M'bago demanded.

"I am your judge and executioner," Rority replied sternly. "You will answer for your sins."

"Bailiff, Arrest that man!" M'bago demanded.

"You must not touch me, lest you turn to stone," Rority replied sadly, wishing he had his stratodoober so he could get stoned.

He quickly programmed the nobots that constituted his shield to change the tissues of the attackers' flesh to calcium; not the amounts needed for muscles to work, but solid calcium. Skin as well as muscle. The bailiffs reached out to grab him, and at the first touch of the nobots that ensheathed Rority they apparently became clothed statues, their brains unchanged but dying from lack of oxygen. It would not have been a pleasant death.

"Serves the bastards right", Rority thought. But he had to stay true to character.

"You have had pestilence, violence, famine, and death these past four years. You have been visited by those four horses, and are paying and will continue pay for your sins for the rest of your natural lives. You will then die, dead forever, and the dead shall live."

"Bullshit!" shouted one man. "Four horses, God, resurrection, it's all bullshit. There is no god, God damn it!"

"Please forgive us!" screamed another man, falling on his knees.

"It is too late. You have already been judged" Rority replied sadly.

"But I was a Catholic! I went to church every Sunday! I went to confession!" the man on his knees pleaded.

"The sins you confessed to were not the sins you were judged for. The sins all of you committed were the same sin – the sin of blasphemy. All of you worshiped false gods."

"No! I never..."

"The god you worshiped, what you loved more than your family, even more than God, more than anything else, was money and power over your fellow man. You bribed judges, policemen, government officials. You threw innocent people out of their homes, let them go hungry and without medical care, all so you could live lavish lifestyles.

"Men like you put people in prison for growing a plant, and by the way one of my favorite plants, too." Rority's research into why the simulated policeman had tried to arrest him at the simulated D'Arcy's had pissed him off. He'd accepted this assignment gleefully, Gumal with the greatest reluctance.

"You executed men for murders that you knew they were framed for, just to obtain advancement in your occupations. You waged terrible wars in the name of God for your own selfish ends."

One of the bailiffs pulled out his pistol and shot at Rority. The bullet ricocheted off of his nobotic shield, although it did smart a little. Those damned bullets were hot!

The bailiff's mouth sagged open, he looked around, pointed the gun at his own head and fired, blood and tissue spraying everywhere, and he collapsed on the floor.

Rority touched the still profusely bleeding wound, and the nobots entered and repaired the damage. He touched the other two dead bailiffs, who collapsed as well. All three were breathing again, but unconscious.

"You shall seek death, but shall not find it," Rority said.

"You will spend the rest of your lives serving those who were formerly poor. The tattoos you put on your own foreheads and hands are the sign of the wicked, and men will be commanded to stay away from you." By then the assembled group were sobbing uncontrollably.

Rority vanished.

Well, he didn't vanish really, he simply activated his nobot cloak to become invisible and walked out through the door toward the church.

The nobots had landed and started working right after the asteroid had hit, producing more nobots by the quintillions. They had been repairing the dead tissues of the plants, and they were already producing fruit.

The decayed corpse that had been laying in the dust for years began looking more and more human as the nobots repaired the dead tissue. It fluttered its eyes and sat up.

"Are you... are you Christ?" the man asked.

Rority just smiled and said "What did you do in life?"

"My name's Jim Hanson. I was a coal miner."

"Not any more," Rority told him.

"Then what am I to do?"

"Whatever you want."

"Then this is... is this heaven?"

Rority smiled. "I guess it is, Jim!" he said.

"What about my brother?" Hanson asked, worried.

"What did he do, Jim?"

"He was an astronomer."

"That's good! He'll be up in a while. Were you married, Jim?"

"Yes," he replied, "she was a waitress. But she died ten years ago."

Rority smiled. "She'll be here soon, too. You're going to be together."

This trip had turned out well.

On his way back to ten million years into the future, or what was the future from when he left, Rority stopped off earlier in 50 AB for a few cases of Guinness as the nobots worked to return him to human form again.

The clerk looked up as the automatic door to the convenience store he worked in opened. Nobody was there, why did the door open?

As he was putting his headphones on to listen to music, he saw a cooler door open. Was someone in here? He walked toward the cooler, and the automatic door opened again.

It happened several times.

Odd. He'd have to tell his boss about the door malfunction... nah. That's his problem. As to the cooler door, well, maybe he shouldn't be smoking pot at work. At least not so much.

He put his headphones on and cranked the Zeppelin.

After returning, Gumal dropped by Rority's place, saying "I guess this is cause for celebration. We're still here!"

"You knew we would be, or we'd never have existed. Here, have a beer," he said, and handed Gumal a Guinness.

Rority took a toke off his stratodoober, and Gumal sipped his beer, which promptly slipped out of his hand and broke on the ground.

"God damn it!" Gumal exclaimed.

"Uh, you already did, didn't you?"

Chapter 10

Blood on the Plow

Reverend Smith walked down the dusty lane towards the Muldoons' place, worrying about tomorrow's sermon.

He didn't have one.

He'd been praying for inspiration all week, and had come up dry. He had been visiting his flock that day, thinking maybe inspiration would come that way. So far, no luck. He prayed some more as he walked.

The Jameson boy had taken ill, but it was nothing serious. He'd visited the family, prayed with them, and walked on. He still didn't have a sermon.

He decided to visit the Muldoons, and walked towards their farm, continuing to pray for a miracle.

Rebekkah heard the pained screams and ran toward them, worried sick about her beloved husband. She ran past the planted field, and through the partly plowed field, and there Jonah lay, grasping his leg, blood squirting out of it with every heartbeat. By the time she reached him the deeply tanned farmer had lost consciousness and was as pale as a newly bleached bed sheet.

Jonah's mule and plow were nearby, the plow in a pool of blood that stretched to where Jonah lay.

She tore off a piece of her skirt to make a tourniquet out of and applied it, but she feared it was too late. He'd lost a lot of blood! He got more and more pale, and his breathing became more and more shallow.

Her husband was dying. She was sure of it. She knelt down and prayed that the Lord God would save him. "We're so young, Lord! We don't even have a child yet! Please, please, Lord, don't take him from me!

"But Lord," she added, "Thy will be done, not mine. In Yeshua's name I pray, Amen."

She opened her eyes and saw... well, she wasn't sure what she saw through her tears. She wiped them out of her eyes and saw the Reverend Smith bending over Jonah. "Rebekkah, what happened here?! All this blood!" he said.

"I don't know, John. I was churning butter when I heard him scream. By the time I got here he was unconscious. I put a tourniquet on, but..." she sobbed "I'm afraid I was..." she sobbed again, "too late!"

"My poor child," said the Reverend, his hand on her shoulder. "Dear Lord, if it be your will, please spare Jonah, and please comfort this poor child in her time of grief. In Yeshua's name I pray, amen."

Jonah groaned, and Rebekkah startled. "Jonah?"

Jonah looked a little less pale. His eyes fluttered open. "Oh, Christ, my leg!" he panted. "Oh God, it hurts! And I'm so thirsty!"

Smith's eyes opened wide. "Jonah? Are you all right?"

"Reverend? When did you get here? No, I'm not the least bit all right! My leg... the plow almost cut it off! It really, really hurts! Oh, God!" he said, gasping. "I think I'm going to die!"

"You just lie still, Jonah," the preacher replied. "Rebekkah, stay here with him while I go get some help." He then took off running.

When he returned with three other men and a stretcher, Jonah was upright, with his wife helping him walk back to their house. "Jonah?" Reverend Smith said, "I brought strong drink, as it says to in the holy book's book of Proverbs."

"Thank you, Reverend, but it doesn't hurt as much. I think the bleeding stopped, but I need water. Yeshua but I'm so thirsty!"

"But how... thirty minutes ago your leg was half off!"

Jonah smiled, took a step, and grimaced. "It's a miracle, John, truly a miracle. Praise be to God! Shall we all go to my house and commune with a glass of wine?"

"Well," said the reverend, "Forgive me, Lord, but I could use a stiff drink!"

He knew what his sermon was going to be tomorrow.

Chapter 11

The Assassin

"Good thing Williams isn't here tonight," O'Brien said.

"Why's that?" Johnson asked.

"I have ten clams in the pool. If he lasts two more days then hacks, I'll win the pot!"

"What pot? How come I never got in on it?"

"See McDaniels, you may still be able to get in, I don't know. Just don't let that gunghole Zales hear about it or we'll all go on report for gambling on duty."

Johnson grinned. "On duty? I don't see you holding any money!"

O'Brien laughed. "Yeah, well, we'd get out of it but then Maris would have to have a say, and I don't know how the Lieutenant would react. So keep it under your shoe, OK?

"Anyway," he continued, "Just see McDaniels."

The screen was instructive. "Yep, he'd hack tonight, all right - Ford's bar hopping," O'Brien said. "Ten clams says it won't be ten minutes before we see brainy Venusians."

Johnson gave him a quizzical look. "Brainy how?"

"Brainy as in brains all over the walls."

Johnson laughed. "Nope, not gonna take that bet!"

"Wise," said O'Brien, laughing even louder than Johnson. "He just killed some guy that was only just standing there.

On screen, Washington holstered his pistol as the Venusian's headless corpse hit the floor, twitching and flailing and squirting blood all over the room and not being the least bit polite at all, making such a nasty mess and not saying "Hark!" and all that.

The bartender yelled “Hark!” The patrons echoed “Hark!”

“That's better,” Washington grumbled.

“Galaxy,” O'Brien swore in disgust. “Uh, oh...”

A Venusian in the back of the tavern had a gun in his hand.

“BOOM!” it roared as Washington's coat sparked and the man next to him fell, clutching his side. The man who had fired the pistol screamed “That was my brother you killed, you son of a bitch!”

“OW!” Yelled Washington, the bullet having ricocheted off his carbon fiber suit, hitting the man who was now laying on the floor bleeding. Washington whirled around, his own gun in his hand. The man who had shot him aimed and shot again, the bullet again ricocheting and hitting a different patron, who also fell to the floor bleeding.

Washington adjusted a control on his gun, pulled its trigger, and the would-be assassin fell to the ground, screaming in agony from his third degree burns.

“Security!” Washington ordered. “Chain him in the dungeon. He's to be crucified in the morning and his family is to all be publicly beheaded as he's forced to watch before he's nailed up. Keep that damned traitor alive!

“Now,” he said, turning back to the bar. “Another! Make it a double! And one for this poor fellow laying here bleeding... oh, never mind, he's dead.”

“Oh, for Mars' sake!” O'Brien said, frowning in disgust. “I'd rather clean toilets with my hands than watch this shit.”

Johnson laughed. “That's what Zales said about reading your reports!”

“Funny,” replied O'Brien sarcastically. “Ha ha. I'll bet he hangs on every word of yours,” he said.

Washington finished his drink, left the bar, and got into his limousine. “Boeing, Building F-74.”

“Yes, sir,” said the driver.”

"Oh, hell," said O'Brien. "This is really not good. Washington never goes anywhere but home after bar hopping. I'd better watch this close."

"Hey, Greg!" he said to Johnson, "Keep an eye out, something's up."

"What's up, Larry?" Johnson answered. "They assigned Ford to me, and he's sleeping."

"Washington's going to a rocket facility after bar hopping. He's up to something."

"A rocket facility? After bar hopping?"

"Phobos phobia yeah, twentieth facility in a week. I wonder what that crazy ghoul has up his sleeve?"

"Sarge!" said Johnson. "You're early."

"I had a funny feeling something was up," the Sargent said.

"Something is," O'Brien reported. "I don't know what, though. Washington's in another spaceport."

"No idea yet what's up?" asked Zales.

"Negative, Sarge. It's almost like he thinks the Shambler is watching him!"

"Shambler? What's that?" Johnson asked.

"It's from a Venusian folk tale they scare their kids with at bedtime," the Sargent answered. "It's about a big, scary monster that rips children apart with its razor sharp claws and eats them. It's meant to keep them from killing their siblings. 'Do you want the Shambler's claws to visit you tonight?' they'll say when the kid acts up. There's even a nursery rhyme about him. Listen to this:

You better watch out,
You better not cry
Better not pout
I'm telling you why
Shambler's Claws are coming around.

He's smacking his lips
You better be nice,
Or he'll eat you up like a big bowl of rice.
Shambler's Claws are coming around,

He sees you when you're sleeping
He knows when you're awake.
He knows if you've been bad or good,
So be good or you'll be cake!

"No kiddin'?" said Johnson. "Nasty bastards! They do this to their kids? Galaxy!"

"They're certainly not the winners of the parents of the week contest" said O'Brien.

"No kiddin'," Johnson repeated. "Where did you hear it?"

"Watching the screens," Zales said. O'Brien nodded in agreement and said "That's not the worst thing they do to their kids, either. Hey, Sarge, are you stayin'?"

"Might as well, why?"

"Mind if I go home? I mean if you can relieve me..."

"Yeah, O'Brien, I guess. Had enough of Washington, have you? Sure, go on."

"Thanks, Sarge. See ya!"

Johnson said "Can I..."

"Nope," answered Zales.

"Why not, Sarge? You let..."

"There's only one of me. If there were a dozen I wouldn't need you guys."

"Mind if I ask a personal question, Sarge?"

Zales snickered. "You can *ask*."

"Well... well, Sarge, sorry, but why are you so gung-ho?"

Zales smiled. "Long story."

"I got time."

"And personal."

"Oh. Sorry, Sarge."
"Don't mention it."

After work, Zales glowered as he rode his floater home. He would never let anyone know his family secret, the secret he always tried to forget, the secret that Johnson had forced into his thoughts: Angela Picard was his paternal great grandfather.

Angela Picard, the traitor who had cost so many lives a century earlier.

The Sargent had changed his name from Picard to Zales at a young age, and never spoke of his family to anyone.

Nobody hated the Venusians more than Zales.

Chapter 12

Bigfoots

Rority howled with laughter. "You want me to be a *what?*"

"It isn't funny," Rula replied. "If you become a protohuman your brain won't be big enough to understand how to synthesize the Lysergic acid hydroxyethylamide in such a way that it's nontoxic. It's only a single muon's difference in a single atom of one of the carboxamides out of every third molecule. Exact precision is needed. Here, read the report."

In 68 AB a fungal epidemic would have wiped out two years' worth of the north American continent's entire corn and soybean crops. Had it been allowed to do so, the world's food supply would have been in jeopardy, and its already existing monetary recession would have become a global depression of unprecedented scope. The mathematicians said that it would have resulted in the entire timeline being disrupted, with catastrophic results for the present, ten million years later. Humans would have become extinct. Rority would have to use the modified $C_{18}H_{21}N_3O_2$ to combat it.

"So I won't *really* be a Sasquach," Rority said, mulling over the report. "I'll be human with a nobot covering that just makes me look like one. Hmm... this one might interest Gumal; he hates having his cells repositioned and their DNA restructured, but he's gotten very interested in the far ancient past ever since I brought that beer back. It might not be easy to control the nobots, though; my feet won't even reach the ground."

"The nobots will handle it," Rula said. "I'll ask Gumal if he wants in."

"He's inside getting us a beer... here he comes now," Rority said as Gumal walked out of the "house".

"Oh, Hey, Rula! Are you here are are you a nobot simulation?"

Rula grinned. "I'm slumming, you reprobate! I have a new assignment for you and Rority." She handed him a copy of the report, which Gumal promptly read.

"Want a beer, Rula?" Rority asked.

"No thanks, I have some stuff to do. Besides, Gumal's too busy reading to give me one. I'll take a hit off your stratodoober, though."

"So, you want Rority and me to be Bigfoots?" Gumal asked. "In Illinois? Kind of, um, unbelievable to the folks at the time, isn't it?"

"Here, look at this," she said as the nobot report reassembled itself into an ancient newspaper, looking every bit the paper and ink they had used those millions of years ago.

Gumal read out loud. "Messing with Sasquatch may not be such a good idea, by Kevin Tremain. 'There's something amiss in the backwoods of Chatham, something potentially big. Lately there's been talk around certain areas of town of an unusual howling and screeching sound as well as evidence of some very large footprints.

'Since June there have been at least five to six instances of residents discovering or hearing evidence that the infamous Bigfoot may be lurking somewhere in the Chatham community. One case in particular has garnered some attention from local police, as well as a few proclaimed Big Foot experts.'

"You gotta be kiddin' me! This is a real newspaper?"

"Yep, it's a copy of the Springfield State Journal-Register, or an exact nobotic simulation anyway. Speaking of nobotic simulations, what happened to your Butler, Rority?"

"Gumal lost a bet. He has to fetch beer for the next week."

"You two can be so childish!" Rula exclaimed.

"Well hell, Rula," Rority replied, "I'm only five hundred years old. I'm barely grown! And Gumal's only fifty years older!"

"Well, are you guys taking the assignment?"

"Sure," said Rority. "How about it, Gumal?"

Gumal laughed and handed beers to Rority and Rula. Rula repeated "No thanks, Gumal, I have some stuff to take care of."

Gumal said "First we're little green men from Mars and now we're Sasquach! Hilarious, I'm in."

"One more thing," Rula said. "This isn't in the report, but the math boys said that the time distortion that you two are going to go back to fix shouldn't have happened in the first place, but did in fact happen. Someone has distorted the timeline, and we don't know who, what, or when they are and are from, or why they did it. The number guys say it could be something or someone from another dimension, or even from our future. They might not even be human.

"We just don't know, the numbers are wrong. Like rounding errors, which are impossible in real life.

"This one looks easy, but you guys could run into trouble."

"Oh hell," Gumal said, "no big deal. Rority can have the nobots turn him into a protohuman when we're done and he can get more beer. We've only got a couple of cases left."

Rority laughed. "Nice try, asshole, but I don't need to be a protohuman to get beer. I have nobots. I get my beer invisible. Where's my stratodoober?"

Chapter 13

The Hacker

"BLARRRGH!! HACK! Broof Blargggggggg Glug... Oh, galaxy! AAAARGHblugblug HACK Oh, shit! Son of a bitch... Blurg..."

"Williams, take your bag and get some fresh air. Johnson, watch his screens," Zales ordered.

"Sure thing, Sarge," Johnson replied. "Williams must have had a little too much breakfast."

Zales shook his head. "He shouldn't have volunteered for Venuswatch duty if he has a weak stomach."

"Aw, he'll get used to it, Sarge. I had to hit the bag a few times myself when I was as green as him. I lost a little weight since I started."

"I'll go see how he's doing," Zales said. "O'Brien, you're in charge 'til I get back."

"Affirmative, Sarge," O'Brien answered. Zales went outside, and O'Brien said "Whoopie! Looks like I won the pot!"

Johnson said "Lucky you! Man, these Venusians sure are some sick bastards. I can see why Williams hacked, watching this sure isn't giving me an appetite."

"That's why I watch sports when I get home from work," said O'Brien. "It takes my mind off of this disgusting job! Did you see the zooterball game last night?"

"No, I had to work on my floater. Damned levitator went out again. I'm going to have to have a mechanic adjust it."

"My floater's been acting up, too, probably the levitator, same as yours. I'm glad I won that pot, it'll go a long way towards paying off the mechanic because I'm sure it's going out of adjustment. With my luck my mechanic Bob will probably say I need to replace the whole damned thing, that floater's pretty old.

"Bob says the Pist levitators are junk that have to be adjusted every six months, and you need special tools that you can't just print out to do it with, you have to buy them from Pist. When it needs another adjustment I'll probably have him put a self-adjusting Heinlein on it and trade in the Pist. I shouldn't have any more problems after that."

"A Heinlein? Those suckers are expensive!"

"Yeah, but the Pist is false economy. As cheap as a Pist is, having it worked on every six months is expensive, and what the tools cost would buy five Heinleins."

Johnson made a face and said "I can't afford a Heinlein. I'm still paying off the Pist and the rest of the floater it's installed in."

"But you can afford to pay a mechanic every six months? They don't work for cheap, either, you know. The expensive tools and other equipment they have to buy makes them have a lot of overhead. Everybody thinks floater mechanics are all rich, but Bob showed me his books. Poor guy's deep in debt and works his ass off for peanuts. Pist rips those guys off worse than they do his customers."

Johnson said "I can afford to pay a mechanic all at once, but I can't afford to shell out what a Heinlein costs all at once and I don't want to borrow any more money."

"Hell, Greg, the Heinlein will pay for itself in three years including interest on the loan. Why *not* take out a loan?"

"I probably will next year when I get the floater paid for... if nothing else goes wrong with it. I wonder how Williams is doing?"

O'Brien laughed. "I'll bet he fell in love with a ghoul woman!"

Johnson looked a little ill. "That's disgusting, Larry. You suck at comedy. Don't give up your day job!"

O'Brien grinned. "Tough room," he said.

Outside, Zales put his hand on Williams' shoulder. "Feelin' a little better, son?"

"Yeah, Sarge. Galaxy but those creatures are nasty!"

"I can't argue with that, Williams. What made you hack?"

"Well, I was watching Washington. He went in to a bar called..." Williams frowned. "The Dead Martian."

"Surely that didn't set your stomach off."

"No, but the first thing he did was cut off three Venusians' heads with that gaudy sword, they must have looked at him funny or something. That was bad enough, the way their eyes blink and their mouths open and close like they're trying to breathe, while the body and limbs flop around with all that blood squirting out of the neck!"

"You'll see worse than that," Zales admonished.

"It did get worse. He laughed, downed some kind of drink, and propositioned a woman. When the Venusian she was with objected, Washington blew the guy's head of with his microwave gun."

"And that's when you got sick?"

"Hell, no, Sarge, that didn't even make me queasy. That ghoul almost had me laughing when he was flopping around without a head.

"After Washington blew the guy's head off, the woman yelled 'Who wants a blow job?' Three guys stood up and she microwaved them. She and Washington thought it was hilarious.

"Then they both got naked and had sex right there on the bar table in front of everybody. And then..."

"Yeah?"

"I guess she was having an orgasm. She screamed out 'oh, yeah! Oh yeah! I feel like my head is going to explode!'

"So then he shoots her in the head with his microwave, and her head exploded, and..."

Williams heaved into his bag again. "Sorry, Sarge. Anyway, *he kept humping her headless, twitching body!*"

Zales looked a little ill himself. “Look, George, we have plenty of staff today, go ahead and take the afternoon off.”

“Thanks, Sarge,” Williams said. “If somebody kills that sick bastard I want to see the video.”

“Sure thing. Get some rest, watch a ball game or something. You're probably going to need to eat, I think your breakfast is in that bag.”

“Hell, Sarge, I may never eat again!”

Zales laughed. “Yeah, I know what you mean. You'll be OK in a while. Go home and get some rest before everybody else starts hacking.”

“Thanks, Sarge. See you in the morning.”

“See you. And Williams...”

“Yeah?”

“Don't eat so much for breakfast tomorrow!”

“I think I'll skip breakfast tomorrow, Sarge. See you.”

“See you, Williams.”

“God, I hate this job already,” Williams said silently to himself.

Chapter 14

Terry and the Nac Mac Feegle

Terry opened his bleary eyes, wondering what he was doing at a desk. Then he remembered – he'd been doing his homework, and must have fallen asleep at the boring drudge.

"Dumb teachers," he thought. She'd marked a paper of his down for "incorrect" spelling. G olo G and jee ogre fee weren't acceptable ways of spelling those words, it seemed. He got a little cross at that – she should have given him an A for creativity. What would she know, anyway? Never trust anybody older than ten!

"Oi there, laddy."

Terry jumped, fully awake now. "Who..." he started, "*What* are you?"

"Oim a Nac Mac Feegle. An' yer Terry, oincha?"

Terry stared, his mouth hanging open. A little red haired man no more than six inches high, wearing a kilt, was talking to him. "You sound Irish," he said, "are you a leprechaun?"

"WHAT?!?!" the little man exclaimed angrily. "Leprechauns are Oirish, Oim Scoottish. Doon ya noo the differ'nce between a Oirish kilt and a Scootish kilt? Doon' they teach yer anythin' in yer schools?"

"Um, maybe a fairy?"

This just made the little man angrier. "Noo! fairies are pixies. We're pictsies. We're Nac Mac Feegles, noo 'leprechauns'. Noo listen, laddy, there's somethin' important yer gotta do when yer a bit oolder. Quite a bit oolder in fact."

"Oolder? Don't you mean older?"

"Doon sass me, boy, oov course oi mean oolder. Doon' they teach ye kids anythin' anymore?"

"Well, I have stupid teachers who mark my papers down because I don't like the way some words are spelled and I spell them any way I want to."

"Noo wonder yeer ignorant. Eenyway, what yer gotta do is just remember tonight."

"Why?"

"Yer just do. An' remember the magic!" he exclaimed as the pencil changed into a snake and slithered away.

Rority giggled as his Nac Mac Feegle, made out of nobots of course, ran away from Terry and scurried under the door. "Man I love his books!" Rority said.

Lets see, the next protohuman on his list was a fellow named Jay Are Are. He'd have to be introduced to... Rority checked the list... Dwarves? Why dwarves?

Oh well. He started his timeship and flew off, giggling some more, and took another toke off his stratodoober.

Rority loved his work.

Chapter 15

Rocket Man

"Mornin', Sarge."

"Mornin' Williams. How are you feeling today?"

"I'm fine today, Sarge. Got pretty hungry by last night."

"I hope you didn't eat too much this morning."

Williams laughed. "I skipped breakfast. I'm starving, but I'll bet I won't be the least bit hungry in a while. Those are some really sickening animals, Sarge. Literally sickening. Really. I can't understand how they can keep their society together."

Zales chuckled. "You call what that scum sucking bunch of ghoulish bloodthirsty sons of bitches who live on that nasty shitball of a planet have a 'society'?"

"No, what I mean is, how does Washington get away with it?"

"He pretty much owns the planet."

"Yeah, I know, but I would think that somebody in that bar would have stood up for himself rather than having his head explode, or cut off with that gaudy sword. I can't understand why he's never been assassinated and why they don't revolt."

"They do have revolutions sometimes, how do you think Washington got to be in charge? And what would you prefer, a quick, relatively painless death, or death by the most excruciating forms of torture? Have you seen the skeletons hanging on crosses around the palace?"

"Yeah, those Venusians sure have a funny sense of decoration."

“They’re not just decoration, they’re warnings. Those are Venusians who attempted either assassination, or revolt. There was an attempted assassination not too long ago, and that guy's hanging up outside the palace right now. He might even still be alive.

“Crucifixion is the most painful way there is to kill someone. In ten million years nobody's come up with anything more painful. Nails driven into the hands and feet go through areas with little blood flow, but lots of nerves. And they can hang there, in pain from the nails through all those nerves, pain in their chests from the attempt to breathe normally, without food and without water for days until they actually die.

“With the Venusians it takes even longer because of the drugs they give them before they crucify them. And not only do the drugs make them take longer to die, the drugs are engineered in such a way that the drugs themselves introduce even more pain, disable endorphin receptors, and deplete the brain of serotonin.

“And they’re pre-tortured before the crucifixion. Be glad we don't have to watch that! Believe me, you don't want to see it.

“Then there’s the civil aspect,” he continued. “They’re hated. People throw rotten vegetables and feces and urine and other things, the nastier the better. If they actually kill the poor bastard hanging up there by, say, throwing a rock, penalties are pretty severe. They want them to suffer, suffering like you or I could never imagine, for as long as possible.

“The populace doesn’t have weapons as good as them. You saw how Washington cut heads off with his sword? Normal Venusians don’t have swords like that; Washington’s sword would slice right through a civilian sword. Civilians’ swords probably wouldn’t even behead you.

“The non-military people don’t have microwave pistols, either. All they have is pellets propelled by a chemical explosion. They can be deadly if the victim doesn't get medical help quickly, but any soldier shot by one would be fine later, even though the poor moron that shot him wouldn't."

"Wow," said Williams.

"Yeah, wow," agreed Zales. "Anyway, it's about time for the shift to start. When you get to your workstation, you'll have it a little easier than yesterday. You don't have to watch Ford or Washington, I'm assigning you a couple of rocket facilities instead. Nobody should have to watch the horror you saw yesterday, every day. It would drive a man insane."

"Thanks, Sarge."

"Don't mention it. Uh, have a bag handy just in case. The rest of those damned ghouls can get pretty ugly, too."

Williams sauntered over to his workstation, ready to relieve O'Brien. "Hey, Larry, bad night?"

"Not really," O'Brien said. "Actually it was a light shift, Washington only killed one guy. How are you feeling today? You looked pretty damned pale yesterday."

Williams blushed. "Yeah, well, I didn't expect necrophilia. I can't figure out why he shot her, aren't those bozos always trying to procreate?"

"Well, yeah, but the same thing had happened a week earlier with the same woman, that's where she got the blaster. Washington gave it to her as a gift. He killed her because she wasn't faithful. Washington doesn't want to be cuckolded."

"Ain't like Washington's faithful."

"Of course not. He doesn't have to be, he's dictator. He *owns* Venus, it's his, as well as everything and everybody on it. He wants to spread his semen to as many women as possible. And he can, because he runs the world. *Owns* the world."

"I still don't get how their society doesn't fall apart. Where does the food come from? The machinery? The power generation?"

"Most of it is automated. I mean, how many farmers do we have here on Mars? We have one guy who directs everything, and the machines do the rest. It's the same on

Venus only not nearly as advanced as our technologies, they still need quite a bit of labor. Hell, we gave them most of that automation and they stole the rest of what they have.

“Then there’s their prisoners. As violent as ghouls are and as overpopulated as Venus is, if they didn’t need workers every unlawful act would be a capital offense. But, you know, if we hadn't helped them after that last war they'd probably be extinct by now.”

“Isn’t the Sarge going home?” Williams asked.

“Are you kidding me? He’s the most gung-ho guy in the Martian army! Suits me, he actually likes watching the screens and I hate it. If he went home I’d have to stay overtime and watch 'em. Can’t for the life of me figure out why his wife doesn’t leave him, he’s here more than home.”

“Maybe him not being there much is what keeps his marriage together,” Williams said. “I hear Zales wants to just nuke Venus and be done with it.”

“Yeah, but it isn’t up to the military, let alone some lowly Sargent. It’s up to the government psychologists. One of them explained why we couldn’t on a newscast I saw once, but it didn’t make much sense to me.”

“Yeah, I saw that, too, and it didn't make much sense to me, either.

“Oh crap, look at that! I’d better keep a closer look at this screen,” Williams exclaimed excitedly.

“I thought you just had a rocket facility? Not much going on.”

“No, but I have to watch it, anyway. Five screens worth. And it looks like Washington showed up.”

On Williams’ screen, Washington was speaking to his underling in the facility. “This is top secret. You are to discuss this with no one, not even General Ford. Got it?”

“Yes, sir. What are my orders sir?”

“Get ten more warships ready.”

“Yes sir,” said the underling. “Where are we sending them, sir?”

"Not yet, Colonel, this is strictly on a need to know basis. We think there are spies. Now, dismissed!"

"Yes sir," said the Colonel, saluting.

"Damn," said O'Brien, still standing by Williams' screen. "I thought we might learn something!"

Williams sighed. "That ain't my kind o' luck. I never catch a break!"

"Well," said O'Brien, "at least he didn't cut the guy's head off and fuck the corpse. That's a lucky break, isn't it?"

"I guess," said Williams. "Galaxy but this job sucks!"

Chapter 16

Hadron Destroyers

“I don't know,” Rority said, “maybe this time we stopped them?”

“Fat chance,” replied Gumal. “You know history says they kept at it until it worked.”

“Yeah, Gumal, but it was supposed to have been permanently offline when we put that bird on the wire.”

“Look, I don't want to go back there again!”

“Maybe you won't have to.”

“I mean, it really *sucks* there,” Gumal whined. “They have *weather*. Real weather! It gets cold, and hot...”

“Yeah, Gumal, but it doesn't get very hot where you're going.”

“It does compared to here!”

“Yeah? It could be worse,” Rority said, “you could be going to Neptune. Or Mercury. Just wear your suit.”

“The suit doesn't stop those damned people from being assholes. What if someone shoots at me?”

“It'll hurt. So what?”

“Yeah, but it'll HURT! You ever been shot with one of those things? God but it hurts! It burns like hell!”

“Hurt? It's just a metal projectile and you have nobots. Pussy!”

“Yeah, lets see how pussified you get if you get shot! The slug is made of lead and launched by a chemical explosion, and the projectile itself is as hot as a frying pan from the explosion.”

“Yeah, I know, I've been shot but the nobots make the projectiles bounce off. It does smart a little from the heat of the projectile, but it doesn't hurt that bad. Pussy!" he said again. "But what's a frying pan?"

"Oh, it's a cooking thing my grandpa uses when we go camping. It's a really quaint antique, more than antique. It makes the food taste funny."

"How is it heated?"

"You set it on a fire."

"Damn, that *is* primitive!"

Rula walked in. "Coffee break's over, boys. Time to go back."

"Shit!" Gumal exclaimed. "You checked? I have to go back?"

"Yep. They got the damned thing started again. It's on your monitor over there."

"Fuck. Fuck fuck fuck FUCK!"

"Calm down," said Rority, "this one's easy. You don't even have to go into the facility."

"You got the specs?"

"Yeah. You only have to cause a minor power failure. It should knock out the coolant and prevent them from fixing it for another year at least."

"Yeah? Lets hope the setback isn't minor."

"So they won't confirm the Higgs until that stupid war they're having is over?"

The confirmation of the Higgs had nothing to do with the war, it was a matter of making sure that the things that had happened in the last ten million years had happened in the right order.

Everything is tied together. Every single subatomic particle in the universe is connected to every other subatomic particle in the universe, no matter how weakly, through time as well as through space. If things happen in the wrong order all sorts of entropic problems ensue and they're never fun or pretty, but instead rather strangely weird in a scary kind of horrible way. Rority's and Gumal's jobs were mostly to fix things earlier travelers had distorted.

"No, damn it, I don't care about that damned boson or when they confirm it, I just don't want to have to go back again! I hate it there. It's so... *primitive.*"

Chapter 17

Launch

"Thank you, Sargent," said Lieutenant Maris. "These observations are indeed troubling. Keep a close eye on them. That'll be all. Dismissed."

Zales saluted, turned on his heel as Maris returned his salute, and walked out, closing the door behind him.

"What a gunghole," Maris said to nobody in particular, since he was in the room by himself. Still, he thought, the military needed gung-ho men like Zales. Zales had pointed out that the numbers didn't add up, as Maris had seen shortly after the first rocket had launched, and had come to the conclusion that the Venusian mathematicians were idiots. Maris didn't think so.

He picked up his tablet and continued working on the Venusian fleet's trajectory that he'd been working on when Zales had knocked. It was a puzzle. It was apparent that the ships weren't headed for Mars or Earth, and he had a hard time figuring out where they really were going, and had little idea at all where or why. Not any idea that made any sense, anyway. So he studied the math.

He doubted they would hit the sun, as Zales had insisted they would.

Private O'Brien came in the building as Zales left Maris' office. "Mornin', Sarge," he said. "Did you see the game last night? It was really a good one. Musial made the best play I've ever seen!"

"Good morning, O'Brien. No, I got busy. You're going to be kind of busy today yourself. Here, watch this." He turned on the holoscreen, and the Venusian dictator was giving a speech to his planetmen.

"Fellow Venusians," Washington said in Venusian as the Martian translation crawled across the bottom of the screen. The translation was a necessary redundancy, as part of Zales' and his men's jobs were to be fluent in Venusian.

The Venusian leader continued. "You have all seen the news reports of the uprising in southern Venus. The situation is under control. The traitor Zak and a hundred of his fellow conspirators have been executed for their sabotage. Zak is still alive, hanging on a cross outside the palace. Repairs of the affected facilities are underway, and the affected provinces are under martial law..."

Zales switched off the screen. "Martial law! The stupid Venusians don't seem to realize that Washington owns them and they're all slaves! The 'unrest' is worrying enough as it is, but watch this." He switched the screen back on, and a primitive rocket filled the screen as it lifted off from the surface of Venus, exploding several minutes later.

"We lasered that one from the satellites, and several more, but two got through and actually destroyed two of the satellites we have orbiting around Venus. Two satellites doesn't change our capabilities, but..."

"Yeah, I see," said O'Brien. "Galaxy! Deja Vu. This is how the last system-wide war started. Do you think that the idiots are planning to attack again?"

"Yes, it's a distinct possibility. I'd say yeah, they're being stupid again."

"What did the Lieutenant say about the ones that didn't try to reach the satellites?"

"He didn't say anything to me, but I'm sure he'll pass it up the chain. Keep your eyes open!" he said, putting on his coat.

"You bet, Sarge. That is a bit worrying, even though I don't see how they could possibly be a threat. They don't even have fission bombs, let alone fusion bombs. Sure, they vastly outnumber us but it will never get as far as hand to hand. Their primitive chemical rockets are way too slow to be a threat. They won't get anywhere near Mars before they're destroyed."

"Well, O'Brien, you saw the feed from yesterday; they're overpopulated. Sending a few thousand ships full of thousands of troops each to Mars would ease their overpopulation problem a lot more than an orchestrated civil war on Venus. The problem is, we lost a lot of good people and equipment the last time."

O'Brien cringed. "You know I'll keep my eyes open. See you tomorrow, Sarge."

"See you," said Zales as he walked out.

Johnson was at work manning the screens. "G'mornin', Larry. Venus is up to no good again."

"Yeah, Zales told me we lost two satellites. With all the redundancy we have, two won't matter and we'll have four to replace those two on their way to Venus in a week.

"What's on the screens, anyway, Greg? Looks like there's a new screamer outside the palace. Is the other one quiet yet?"

"Yeah, no sooner did the first one shut up than they nailed up the new one," Johnson said. "The first one tried to kill Washington, but I don't know what the second one did."

"I don't know, either. Washington gave a speech saying it was a minister that sabotaged part of the power grid, but I saw Washington cut that guy's head off. Galaxy, but those Venusians have a lot of blood and it really squirts when they get decapitated. I don't know who they nailed, or why, though."

"Probably some poor stooge that was just following orders. Damned if he did, damned if he didn't, tortured to death either way."

"Oh hell, look at that, they're launching another rocket. A big one, too." He pressed a button on his console.

"Maris here, what's up, boys?"

"Rocket launch, sir. Should we shoot it down?"

"Where's it headed?"

“We don't know, sir. Washington's really being secretive.”

“Is it manned?”

“Yes, sir, it is.”

“How big is the crew?”

“Thousands, sir.”

“Let it go, if it's headed here EL2 will take it out.”

“Yes, sir.”

One of the screens showed the rocket about to lift off, another showing the base commander, a Colonel, watching the launch on his own screen. The huge rocket lifted gracefully off of the launch pad and exploded half a minute later.

Zales walked back in. “Forgot my cobblobbers. Hey, did you guys just shoot down a rocket?” he said, seeing the flaming debris from the explosion raining down on one of the screens.

“No, Sarge,” said O'Brien. “Lieutenant’s orders were to let it fly. It must have had mechanical problems.”

“Yeah,” said Zales, “their junk is junk, all right.

The Venusian Colonel put his pistol in his mouth and closed his eyes tightly before pulling the trigger.

“Stupid ghouls,” O'Brien said. “I wonder who the new screamer's going to be? It sure won't be that one!”

“What difference does it make?” Zales said. “The only good Venusian is a dead Venusian.”

“I don't even like the dead ones,” O'Brien said. “It turns my stomach when one dies.”

“Huh?” Zales said. “Why?”

Johnson said “Excuse me, Sarge, can you watch my screens for a minute? I forgot my lunch and need to call home.”

“Sure, Johnson, go ahead. But be quick, the wife wants me on time tonight.”

“Why?” O'Brien said. “Galaxy, Sarge, because it's fucking disgusting. They all die of natural causes. Disgusting. Just disgusting,” he repeated, not caring about what Zales' wife wanted.

“Natural causes?” Zales said, puzzled.

“Yeah,” said O'Brien. “Natural for a Venusian, anyway. It isn't like any of them ever die of old age. I feel like Williams, I want to hack. I don't know what's worse, the dead Venusian or the one that kills him. Or her,” he said, thinking of the horror Williams had seen, which he had seen countless times himself.

“I never figured you for somebody with a weak stomach, O'Brien,” Zales said.

“I'm not, but Sarge, I hate this damned job.”

“Why don't you resign?”

“The job needs to be done. It sucks, but somebody has to do it. Might as well be me. Better than playing zooterball. Hell of a lot more important, too.”

“Johnson... or was it Williams? Anyway, one of them asked me why I was so gung-ho the other day. That's why. It's important and we need to do it right. By the book.

“Look, O'Brien, you're a good soldier and you're due for a promotion. I'll talk to Maris about it tomorrow.”

“Thanks, Sarge, I really appreciate that!”

“Don't mention it. I mean, really. Keep it under your shoe, OK? Don't even say anything to Dennis.”

“Well, yeah, Sarge, sure. I won't say anything to anybody. Galaxy but I hate this job.”

“Me, too,” said Zales. “Keep that under your shoe, too. What's taking Johnson so long? My wife's going to be furious if I get home late again.”

Chapter 18

The Dance

"Oh hell," Gumal said, taking another sip of his Guinness. "Here comes Rula. Give me another hit off that stratodoober."

"Hi Rula," said Rority. "What's up? Another assignment?"

"Yeah," she replied. "But it's an easy one. I want to try that 'dancing' thing again, but I just don't know enough about the protohumans, especially the ones in the first century A.B. Do you mind?"

"No problem," Rority responded. "I wanted to go get some beer supplies, anyway."

"Beer supplies?"

"Yeah," explained Gumal. "He thinks the problem with the beer he tried to brew was the ingredients. Apparently, hops have evolved in the last ten million years."

"Well, duh," she retorted. "Everything did. At least until five million years ago. I take it you want to bring some hops back?"

"Not just hops," Rority returned, "all the ingredients, even the yeast. If they work out I'll see if the nobots can grow some here and now from seeds or cuttings or clonings or something."

"So," she said, "what will I need for dancing?"

"Uh, your legs?"

"Funny. Ha ha. I mean is there anything I need to learn about the protohumans?"

Rority laughed. "Well, duh indeed. You need to know everything, and I don't. Nobody does, so you just don't worry about it. If you screw something up, you just go back and keep yourself from doing it. The best way to learn is use a nobot shield to be invisible, and just watch them. Want to come along, Gumal? You don't have to go through the genetic displacement; I know how much you hate being a protohuman."

"I don't know... I guess. As long as Rula doesn't make me dance or fall off a building or something. And as long as I don't have to have the genetic manipulation; I hate the weird way it makes me feel so stupid."

"Well, OK! lets go!" Rula said excitedly. "I'm looking for some fun. Where's your timeship?"

Fifteen minutes later they were ten million years earlier, in the air. "So... that's You Nark?" Rula asked.

"No, it's New York," Rority answered. "If you want to learn middle first century dancing, this is the time and place. We want to go to a place here and now called the Radio City Music Hall and watch the Rockettes."

"The rockets?" Rula asked, puzzled.

"No, the Rock*ettes*. They're a dance troup that started about seventy or eighty years before now.

"But before we land, do you see those two especially tall buildings? Well, they're not going to be there long. Both of them are going to fall down this morning. I wish there was something I could do to save the animals."

"What animals?"

"The protohumans who work in the buildings. You know, work to us isn't work to them. We work because we want to. They work because they have to. If they don't work, they have a miserable existence; most of them, anyway. Hell, even most of the ones that work have a miserable existence, but not as miserable as they would if they didn't. There are thousands of protopeople in there, working."

"There was a structural problem in *both* buildings that caused them both to fall at the same time?" Rula asked incredulously. "I know it's incredibly primitive now but..."

"No," Gumal answered. "I don't know as much about protohistory as Rority does, but I know about this one – I've been now before. This is a mass murder done for political reasons."

"Political?" she asked in puzzlement.

"Yeah," Gumal said, "there are some folks who worship Rority who want to take over the world and run it according to their own religion."

"They didn't worship me, dumbass. They worshiped another protohuman named Muhammed," Rority said laughing.

"Well, you're the one who moved the mountain, weren't you? Didn't Muhammed and his followers say that it was Allah who moved the mountain? And isn't Allah the one they worship?"

"Fuck you, Gumal," Rority said, laughing even harder. "Nobots moved the mountain, not me. Using your 'logic' they didn't worship me, they worshiped the nobots." As he spoke, a rather large airborne vehicle smashed into one of the buildings.

"Wow," Rula said. "That was something! Go back, I want to see it again. And, er, shouldn't we stop it?"

"Hell no! I wish we could but our timeline wouldn't exist if we did! And it would be at least twenty four hours before we could go back to fifteen minutes ago, anyway. Maybe longer. But watch the other building, there's another plane that will..." The timeceiver beeped.

"Rority, this is Rority. Are you there?" it said.

"Yeah, me, this is me," Rority said to himself, who was him but not him then. "What's up?"

"I didn't get on the plane!"

"Why not?"

"Not enough time to explain. Look, *You* have to stop that aircraft! If you don't it will kill most of this county's government and we're just *so* screwed."

"OK, I'm on my way," he said, as he adjusted the nobotic controls. "Now, how did you miss the plane?"

"It was your idea, me. OK, I guess it was my idea since I'm you. You know how you hate getting killed. Well, you thought of a better way. Or I did, anyway."

Rority had been tasked with crashing one of the four planes into the ground and was to leave two weeks (present time, ten million years later) later. "Rather than be on the plane, use your timeship to crash it. You're invisible and have plenty of nobots to do the job."

"Why didn't I think of that?"

"You did, after you were yourself again. Well, after I told you anyway. Or after I told me when I was then. You keep forgetting how stupid you are in your present form. Dummy!"

"Yeah, I can barely fly the nobots like this. Tell me what to do. Put some nobots in the engines?"

"No, it didn't crash like that. Listen..."

A short while later they were above Pennsylvania, above a big airplane, with Gumal at the timeship controls, having not been transformed into a barely sentient proto-human like Rority and Rula were.

The pseudo-man, pseudo-woman, and the very short gray time alien with the big head and funny eyes flying the timeship were something no protohuman would see – at least, few would see. The few protohumans who did see humans thought they were from outer space and were believed by nobody, sometimes not even by themselves.

And actually, even though the humans were our descendants, they had to go through space to get to the Earth's past. So maybe they *were* space aliens, especially since time is a dimension and a dimension defines spacial direction, and is curved by speed and gravity like any other spatial dimension.

But I'm just a barely sentient protohuman, what do I know?

The airplane rocked back and forth, with large, invisible nobot structures at the tips of each wing. "It isn't going to work," Gumal said. "The wings of that damned thing might come off. You forget how primitive and delicate this machinery was."

He wished Rority or Rula were in their right minds, and he wished he'd brought a stratodoober so that he wouldn't have to be in his.

"What the hell," he thought, and landed the timeship on the plane's cockpit's roof and pushed it down, letting go right before it hit the ground.

"Wow," Rula said, "That was close!"

Gumal smiled. "How do you like the way I dance?"

Chapter 19

Dennis is a Two Headed Martian

"Honey! I'm home! Dennis, where are you?"

"I'm in the garage trying to get this darned floater to work. The motor's running but it won't float."

"Here, let me have a look," O'Brien said as he kissed his wife. "Hmmm.... Something's wrong with the levitator. I was afraid it was going out of adjustment. We'll have to let Bob look at it, those levitators are pretty hard to adjust properly, impossible without those damned expensive tools. It's a good thing we bought that new floater, we'd be screwed if that old one was the only one we had.

"I was just talking to one of the guys at work the other day, his levitator went out, too. We just had this stupid floater in the shop a few months ago, honey. Do you think we should get a Heinlein for it?"

"A Heinlein? Those are pretty darned expensive!"

"Yeah, that's what Greg said, too, but it's even more expensive getting Bob to adjust the Pist every six months. The Heinleins are self-adjusting and the cost of servicing the Pist in just a few years is way more than what a Heinlein costs."

"Well, I guess. You can take it in tomorrow.

"OK, I will. What's for dinner, sweetie?"

"We're going out to eat – we're celebrating. Larry, honey, we're going to have a baby!"

O'Brien' jaw dropped. "Really? Dennis, that's wonderful!" he exclaimed, a huge smile on his face and tears welling up in his eyes before he started hugging her. "Let me change into some normal clothes," he said. He had come home in his uniform, which he didn't normally do, but he'd been in a hurry.

"How was work, dear?" Dennis asked.

"Awful, just terrible," he said. "Those Venusians are some really vile creatures, just thoroughly disgusting. They're really violent, horribly violent, and they've launched some rockets."

"Oh no! Do you think we'll be at..." she hesitated at the word, and stammered a little. "at w-war?"

"I don't think we have anything to worry about yet, sugar. They might have sent the rockets away from Mars and towards Saturn. Lieutenant Maris gives me the impression he thinks they might be attacking Titan."

"Why Titan? They can't live there."

"Yeah, it doesn't make any sense to me, either. Hey, where are my cobblobbers?"

"I threw 'em out, they were all raggedy. Just print out a new pair!"

"But honey," he whined, "Those were comfortable! I just hate breaking in a new pair!"

"Sorry, sweetie, but I'm not going out in public with you wearing a pair of raggedy cobblobbers. Now print out a new pair and come on, I'm hungry!"

"Yes, dear," he grumbled.

Back on base, his other boss' boss was speaking with his own boss, Colonel Gorn.

"This is disturbing, Maris. Very disturbing," said Gorn.

"Yes sir, it is, and puzzling as well," the Lieutenant replied. "They made a show of attacking our spy satellites and only got two of them, while their warships seem to be going around the sun and *away* from Mars and towards Saturn."

"That's your assessment, Lieutenant?" the Colonel asked, puzzled. "You think they're going to Saturn?"

"Yes, sir," Maris answered. "Maybe they mean to invade Titan. Zales thinks their mathematicians are just stupid, but I think that's highly unlikely. We radioed the Titanians, but of course we don't expect an answer. For all we know, the Titanians could be extinct by now."

"Yes," Gorn said, "You would think the researchers would be looking at our own back yard rather than other galaxies. I wonder why nobody studies interplanetary anthropology?"

"They probably think it's boring, I guess, sir. At any rate, I'll be sending you a full written report."

"Thank you, Maris. That will be all, then."

"Yes, sir," said the Lieutenant, saluting.

"Saturn?" thought Gorn. No, there must be another explanation. Saturn just didn't make sense. Maybe Zales was right and their mathematicians were idiots, but that didn't seem any more likely to him than it did to Maris. Where were they really going? And why?

But Maris had known something was up as soon as the rockets had left Venus' orbit. He was at least right, Gorn saw after Maris had showed him the figures, that there was no way they were headed to Earth or Mars, both at the closest points to each other in their orbits on the other side of the sun from Venus.

O'Brien and his wife were on their way home from their celebratory night out. "Oh, Larry, that was some great food! We need to eat there more often!" Dennis said.

"Yeah," Larry agreed. "Almost as good as your cooking! I can't believe we're going to have a baby. It's scary."

It was actually scarier for a Martian couple than childbirth is to us protohumans. One in a hundred Martians had a pair of recessive genes that when expressed, disallowed the newborn from breathing properly in Mars' thin atmosphere. Scientists said it was a throwback to Martians' Earthly beginnings. It was a hardship on the child, who would have to spend its first decade in a pressure chamber, with a very gradual decompression to normal Martian air pressure.

Many died.

These children never became sports players, something their parents saw as a benefit to these poor youngsters.

"I don't carry the recessive," Dennis said.

"Well, that's good," Larry answered. "I just hope he or she doesn't grow up to be a zooterball player!"

"I guess I'll have to take a sabbatical, Larry. It's really going to pinch our resources."

"It sure will," he replied. "You earn twice what I do, even with my Disgusting Duty bonus. I'll talk to Zales about a promotion, I'm due to make corporal. I'll talk to him tomorrow, and maybe throw a hint or two at Maris as well," he said, keeping his earlier conversation with Zales about it between him and the Sargent.

"At least I'll have your cooking to myself!" he added.

Dennis laughed. "Well, it will be a while before I have to give my job up. But once the baby's born one of us won't be able to work full time. We'll have a child to raise!"

"Well," said O'Brien, "maybe I'll resign when you can go back to work and I'll take care of the baby. I hate my job, anyway."

"Well, that's up to you, dear, but I think your job's important and I don't care what people say. The job sucks, but somebody has to do it. Better than a sports player, nobody really needs to do that job."

O'Brien laughed. "Sports players are unappreciated. They take my mind off my disgusting job," he said as he pulled into the garage. "I hope the mechanic doesn't say that the levitator on that broken floater's shot. Those things are expensive and I need it for a trade in on the Heinlein."

"Talk to Zales tomorrow, Larry. We're going to need the money."

"Yes, dear," he sighed. "I will."

Chapter 20

Titan

"Now, this is strange," Johnson mused.

"What's up, Johnson?" Zales asked.

"The Venusian rockets. They're going *away* from Mars!"

"Let me look... damn. I wonder what's going on. It looked originally like they were coming here! I thought the trajectory was nuts, because they're stupid and their math abilities really suck. I thought they'd smash... uh, never mind."

"Slingshot around the sun, they're going pretty damned fast, straight to Saturn it looks like," Johnson said.

"Saturn? That's what Maris said, but why in the galaxy would they send warships to Saturn?"

"Maybe they're tired of fighting us and want to tangle with the Titanians?"

"Why? Venusians can't live on Titan. There's nothing in the Saturn system they could possibly need. I'd better see the Lieutenant. Where's O'Brien?"

"Dunno, Sarge," said Johnson. "He hasn't showed up. Is he supposed to be on duty today?"

"Damned right he is and he's five minutes late!" As Zales was saying this, O'Brien walked in, beaming.

"Where in the venus have you been?" Zales asked vulgarly. "You're late."

"Sorry, Sarge, dropped by the Lieutenant's office on the way in and he kept me longer than maybe he should have. Have a cigar! You too, Greg."

"Cigar? Dennis is pregnant?" Zales said.

"Sure as Venusians make you want to hack!" said O'Brien.

"Congratulations," said Johnson. "That's damned rare on Mars. You sure you two didn't honeymoon on Venus?"

O'Brien laughed. "Fuck you, Greg!"

Zales stuck out his hand. "Congratulations, Larry. I'll watch your screens if you want to pass some out to the other guys."

"That's OK, Sarge, thanks," O'Brien said, shaking the Sargent's hand, "but I already passed out half a box. What's going on this morning?"

"Maris was right. The Venusian rockets are heading away from Mars."

"Away? They were headed towards the sun a couple of days ago. Greg?"

"Yeah, Larry," Johnson said. "They were doing a slingshot for speed, and are heading to Saturn."

"That's what the Lieutenant said, but I just don't get it," said a puzzled O'Brien. "Why Saturn?"

"Dunno, but... hey, Sarge, weren't you on your way to see the Lieutenant?"

"Yeah," said Zales. "I was. Guess I'd better catch him before he leaves."

Zales walked out, and Johnson snickered. "Maris is going to be pissed. That gung-ho Zales just doesn't get that he's the only one who doesn't want to leave this place. I'll bet the Lieutenant has better things to do than to spend his off-duty hours listening to Zales drone on about Venusians!"

O'Brien laughed. "Yeah, poor Maris! At least he outranks that gunghole and can tell him to shut up. We have to listen to Zales, Maris doesn't."

Johnson laughed. "I need a promotion!"

"Yeah, me too," said O'Brien. "I was talking to Dennis about that last night. I should be up for Corporal pretty soon... hope so, anyway, that's the real reason I stopped by Maris' office on my way in. I wanted to drop a few hints. The baby is going to make things a little more expensive, and Dennis will have to take a sabbatical. Things are really going to be tight."

"Well, Zales will still outrank you. At least unless he pisses Maris off enough to demote him. "

O'Brien laughed. "That gunghole lose rank? Dream on! I don't need to outrank anybody, anyway, I just need the money."

"Well," said Johnson, "you don't *look* like you're short of cash. Those are some really nice cobblobbers you have on! Where'd you get 'em? They look pretty damned expensive. I can't even afford cheap ones, I have to print mine out myself."

"Well, thanks, but I can't afford to buy 'em, either. I printed these out just last night because Dennis threw my old comfortable ones away. Pissed me off.

"And yeah, I need the money. Bob says the levitator on my floater isn't just out of adjustment, it's shot, damn it, so I won't get a trade in. I'm going to have to take out a loan to replace it anyway, so we're getting a self-adjusting Heinlein."

"Damn, sorry. Those Heinleins cost a fortune. But you printed out those cobblobbers yourself? Really? That's a great pattern, those cobblobbers look fantastic! Where'd you get that pattern?"

"Dennis made it. I'll give you a copy."

"Wow, she's good. Thanks! You're lucky, Larry, with such a multi-talented wife."

"You're right about that, she's the best thing that ever hap... oh, hell, I have to watch these screens. Screens, rerun last two minutes and continue."

Two minutes was nothing, depending on where they were in their respective orbits, since signals took a while to reach Mars from Venus, depending on where they were at the time, and the two planets were about as far away from each other as they could get.

"Hark!" the Venusian on the screen said.

"Disgusting," O'Brien said.

"Damn it, Ford, that isn't necessary when it's just us," replied Washington.

"Sorry, General," Ford said. "What are my orders?"

"No orders," said Washington. "The orders have already been given and my plan has been set in place. We'll be rid of the Martians for good!"

"How, sir?"

"Too early. I'll let you know when it's time. Dismissed."

"Yes sir."

"And Ford..."

"Sir?"

"Watch your back. We have spies, we may have assassins as well."

"There are always would-be assassins, General."

"Well, there's one outside!"

"He's still alive?"

Washington laughed an evil laugh. "No, but he's still hanging there, next to Zak's accomplice. I wonder what the two of them talked about while they were still hanging there alive?"

Ford laughed an equally evil laugh. "Yes sir. Any instructions out of the ordinary?"

"No, just know I have a plan set in motion and I don't want you to do anything that may hinder it. Stay away from the rocket ports."

"Yes, sir. I think I'll have a drink, if I've been dismissed."

Washington said "Why not? I'll join you. Come on!"

"Oh, bloody hell," said O'Brien. "I hate watching either one of them in bars. The two of them together? Shit!"

"Sucks to be you," said Johnson. "My shift's over. See ya!"

"See ya, Greg. Oh galaxy, look what those two... YECH!"

Chapter 21

Not a ghost of a chance

"Wacha readin'?"

Rority looked up from his nobotic book at Gumal. "I'm studying programming," he said.

Gumal snorted. "Why? Everybody knows how to program a nobot."

"Wrong," Rority said. "Everybody knows how to program robots and large numbers of nobots, but not individual nobots. It's low level programming I'm studying."

To us protohumans, Rority's learning to program the individual microscopically small machines would be like a protohuman SQL database programmer learning assembly, or even hand assembled machine language, and perhaps even CPU design.

"Why?" Gumal asked.

"Why? Why does Rula want to learn how to dance like a protohuman? In this case, though, I had an idea somebody must have thought of before because it seems trivial to do, but it involves nobot-level programming."

"What?"

It was Rority's turn to snicker. "Jeez, you sound like a protohuman" he said.

Gumal laughed, and replied "fuck you!"

"Now you *really* sound like a protohuman!" They were both in stitches now. I wish I could understand their humor, because they were hilarious – to each other. Me, I just don't get it any more than my cat understands why I'm laughing when she's chasing a laser pointer.

"Well?" Gumal said, still snickering. "What's this big idea of yours?"

"You know how you hate having the nobots do the genetic manipulation that makes you look and kind of think and really feel like a protohuman? I figured out a way for us to look like them without the manipulations."

"Really? How would you go about doing *that?*"

"It's just a step past an invisibility cloak. Rather than each nobot transmitting its input radiation to its opposite's output radiation, the output nobot would vary this, projecting the image of something, but something different than what's behind the cloak; in this case, the protohuman you're falsifying."

"Sounds to me like the math would be a little hard. Have you talked to the number boys and low-level programmers? That kind of thing is fun for them. Me, I hate it."

"Yeah," Rority replied, "I did, and they made a prototype for me. It would fool the average human, but there was something about it that was inprotohuman that I or a real protohuman would have no trouble seeing as fake. So I'm studying programming." He dropped the book, which instantly disintegrated into nobotic dust and disappeared.

"Want a beer?" He asked.

"Yeah, and another toke off your stratodoober," Gumal said. "Look, I have a friend who's a low-level programmer, I'll call her while you get the beer." He held his hand out, and what appeared to be a transparent sheet of thin cardboard appeared in it.

"Ragwel? You there?" He said to the transparent cardboard.

Of course, Rority didn't actually have to go anywhere for the beer; the nobots brought it out.

"Hey Ragwel," Gumal said, "we've been invited to something that's supposed to be really cool. We're going to kidnap a couple of protohumans, then we're partying on Zeta Reticuli. Want in?"

"Well, I don't know," she said. "How many others are going?"

"Half a dozen so far and there are more folks I need to ask. But hey, Ragwel, that's not what I called you about. My buddy Rority has a programming problem."

"Here," he said, handing the "phone" that was as much like a protohuman's phone as a book was to a protohuman's book to Rority. The phone had a holographic simulation of a person's head appearing to be situated just behind the transparent cardboard – or what looked like transparent cardboard. Rority explained the situation to the hologram.

"So," the hologram said, "how, exactly, do the sheaths skew the image? I've been working on the exact same thing you're talking about and it looks to me more of a biological problem than a programming problem."

"Well, it's hard to explain," Rority said. "The colors are a bit off when I've had the genetic manipulations, but they look close enough when I'm myself."

The phone disappeared and a full sized replica of the low level nobot programmer, as well as another simulation appeared.

The simulation of Ragwel said "Meet Kandar, he programs the nobots that reprogram the DNA. He's a molecular cellular biochemistry programmer who studies protohuman biology."

"Hi, er, Rority, is it? Um, you probably didn't notice that colors look different when you're in protohuman form?"

"Uh, no, I didn't. Just that the cloak looked wrong."

"That's because the brain corrects the information it receives, whether a human brain or protohuman brain. Colors are all orangier at sunrise and sunset, but you don't notice it unless you know it's there and notice it *deliberately*. Your brain changes it; the brain is what actually does the seeing. You don't notice the difference between incandescent lighting and fluorescent lighting unless you turn one off and the other one on; you'll probably notice it then."

"What are those?" Ragwel asked.

"Ancient forms of lighting. One simply heated a tungsten filament until it glowed, the other used an electrically generated plasma."

"Clear as mud," the programmer said.

"Well, look," Kandar said to Rority, "the one thing you're doing wrong is using your eyes. Measure the *exact* wavelengths being reflected from the protohumans' skin."

"I did, but the color wasn't right."

"Not right to *you*. It would look right to a protohuman. Like I was trying to tell you, the cones in their retinas weren't exactly the same sizes as ours are, so colors wouldn't be exactly the same."

"OK" said the programmer, doing something on a sheet of nobots. "Try this out."

Gumal said, "You're studying protohuman biology? You'll want to come on that trip we have scheduled."

"Yes, of course I'm going. Well, we'll be seeing you guys."

Rority looked doubtful about the plans Ragwel had given them. "Come on," he said, "lets get Rula and go dancing with the protohumans."

"What if it doesn't work right?"

"Then we'll disappear. Comc on."

On their way to our present, their more than ancient past, Gumal said "Do you really think this will work?"

"I don't know," said Rority. "I'm kind of doubtful. What Kandar said made sense logically, but something tells me it won't work. I can't put my finger on whatever it is, but I'm doubtful. I don't think the color's right."

"Well, we're here," he said after hey had traveled to our time. "We'll go in invisible; they have this thing called a 'cover charge' and I didn't counterfeit any money. When we're inside we'll change the nobots' outputs when nobody's looking. Come on!"

Candice was coming out of the restroom when she saw the three of them and dropped her purse; these were some startlingly weird looking people that had seemed to come out of nowhere. Their features looked markedly African, almost caricatures of African features, but their skin was whiter than a Caucasian who had spent ten years in a Norwegian prison. She screamed when they disappeared before her eyes, then she fainted.

A few minutes later firemen showed up with electronic noises blaring loudly from their bright red vehicle, even though there was no fire. Rority, watching invisibly, wondered if he would ever learn enough about these creatures to really understand them. He had a pretty good handle on the ones before zero BB, but the ones in the wired centuries puzzled him. They were a real challenge, and a big part of what he loved about his job.

Gumal and Rula just wondered how they could actually survive like that.

The firemen had crude protohuman medical tools and took measurements of the bodily functions of the woman who had fainted and who was still unconscious.

More protohumans noisily showed up with electronic sounds screaming at high decibels from their vehicle, just as the firetruck had.

Rority still couldn't figure out why they'd sent a firetruck. He knew what an ambulance was, and what a firetruck was, but it was weird that the medical personnel would be firemen and not the ambulance guys.

These were some strange animals. He loved studying them. Perhaps he could establish a new field of study? Or even more than one!

The ambulance drivers (why were there two?) and the firemen put her on a wheeled cot and took her to the ambulance, which promptly left with her in it, its electronics screaming as noisily as when it had arrived.

The firetruck left as well, having not fought a single fire.

"Fascinating," Rority thought.

Rula was dancing with the protohumans, none of whom could see her because of the nobotic cloak. She was enjoying herself immensely, strenuous as it was.

Gumal sat by himself, bored stiff.

Candice came to in a hospital bed.

"There were three ghosts!" she exclaimed to her friend Willard. "They startled me. It was almost like they just appeared instead of me just not paying attention, then they all three just disappeared in a kind of a shimmer right before my eyes!"

"Nonsense," said Willard. "There ain't no such things as ghosts. I'm getting you a psychiatrist – you must have been hallucinating. Are you on drugs or something?"

"You know better than that. Maybe Halloween got me worked up. I thought they were just in weird costumes and makeup before they disappeared.

"But, well, I guess a shrink wouldn't hurt, that really shook me up!"

Chapter 22

Suicide Bombers

Colonel Smith was worried. Very worried. More than worried.

He was scared halfway out of his mind.

His staff was way behind schedule. The rocket was supposed to have been launched months earlier with the rest of the fleet, but glitch after glitch had kept it on the ground. Washington had given him until today to get it on its way, but there was still a minor fuel leak.

Leak or no leak, it was do or die... literally. Washington had made it clear to him that not only was failure unacceptable, it would cost Smith his life, and cost it in a very painfully unpleasant way. He paced nervously as the countdown played out over the loudspeakers.

"T minus five minutes," the loudspeakers spoke loudly, blaring their echoes through the facility.

Johnson was watching from Mars, glad Zales hadn't given him the task of watching that disgusting pair, Washington and Ford. Just thinking about those two monsters made his stomach churn. "Forget those two and watch your screens," he told himself. "They're not your problem tonight.

"Now pay attention, damn it!" he said to himself.

The Sargent came in, having been busy briefing the Lieutenant about the latest pending launch. "How's the countdown, Johnson?" Zales asked.

"Five minutes to go. What did Maris say? Are we going to shoot it down?"

Zales sighed. "Unfortunately The Lieutenant says no.

“The rest went around the sun and are streaking towards Saturn, and he says this one is probably following the rest of the fleet. He says the technical problems we reported to him probably kept it from launching when the rest of the fleet took off, but if the rest were just a distraction while this one attacked we can knock it down from one of our posts at one of the Earth's Lagrange points.

“How many crew are on that rickety thing?” O'Brien asked.

“Five thousand,” Zales said.

“Galaxy, that's as big a force as our entire military.”

“Damned right,” agreed Johnson. “Of course, their weapons are no match for ours. If they're on their way here they're on their way to their deaths.”

“A lot of Martians died during the last Venusian war,” Zales said. “Hundreds. Of course, the Venusians lost their entire force, hundreds of thousands, but those hundreds of Martians cost Mars dearly. I'll bet if those bastards do attack, Mars will have a lot better opinion of soldiers.”

“Still,” O'Brien said, “I'd rather be looked down on than be at war.”

“T minus one minute,” the screen said, with the loudspeakers echoing loudly through the facility.

Smith was still pacing nervously, trembling a little, with sweat running down his cheek and his metallic skin looking like aluminum.

“T minus thirty seconds.”

A plume of smoke wafted from the bottom of the rocket.

“T minus ten... nine... eight... seven... six... five... four... three... two... one... ignition... liftoff. We have liftoff.”

The rocket rose gracefully off the launch pad as Smith heaved a huge sigh of relief.

It then exploded in a gigantic fireball, and the building shook violently from the Venus-shaking blast.

Colonel Smith unholstered his revolver, put the barrel in his mouth, and pulled the trigger. Blood and brains splattered everywhere.

Zales laughed. “I feel sorry for the poor slob that's second in command!” he said.

“I don't get it, Sarge,” said Johnson. “Why did he do that?”

“Better than crucifixion,” Zales said.

“They'd crucify him for failure?”

“No, they'd crucify him for sabotage.”

“They'd think he did it on purpose?”

“No, but that's what the propaganda would be. They don't want the populace to know they're launching primitive junk. As far as most Venusians know, the Venus military's equipment is well engineered, intelligently designed, well built, and state of the art. Their ignorance is Washington's bliss.”

On Venus, Lieutenant Colonel Donnoly was injecting himself with a strong narcotic. As he let the tourniquet loose and the drug flowed through his veins and the rush went up his spine he knew he would never wake up.

Not waking up was, of course, the whole point of the injection. Someone was going to be tortured to death, and it wasn't going to be him. He intended to die peacefully in his sleep, sitting right there in his chair, and he didn't care what was going to happen to his family. He wasn't going to be crucified no matter what horror befell anyone.

His family was going to go through hell, but he had no intention of joining them there.

Washington and Ford were watching the liftoff and explosion from the palace. “Sabotage!” they both said in unison.

Washington picked up his talker. “Rocket base Argo, base security,” he said to the device.

“Security, Lieutenant Colonel Ogden here. How can I help you, sir?”

“This is General Washington, Ogden. I want all flightline, liftoff, and mechanical personnel arrested, as well as the highest ranking officer on the base.”

“Y-yes sir, General. Right away, sir! Is that all, sir?” he asked, trembling.”

“Yes, Colonel. That is all.”

The Colonel disconnected, pulled out his pistol, and put the barrel in his mouth. Smith and Donnoly were surely dead, and he wasn't about to take responsibility for this clusterfuck of a fubar.

Zales leaned back and laughed. “My kind of enemy!”

“Huh?” said Johnson.

“The best kind. They save us a lot of ammo, doing our jobs for us. Why don't you get us some coffee, Johnson, I'll watch your screens. I'm enjoying this! Lets see, who's next?”

Chapter 23

The Time Triangle

"Hey, Rority, Garmin gave me a new assignment, want to go along?"

"When is it and what do I have to do?" Rority asked suspiciously. "I just turned down an assignment Rula wanted to give me." He had turned the assignment down because he *liked* the protohumans, some of whom were surprisingly almost sentient. He was to some of them like one of the protohumans who leave food and water on the porch for feral house cats. They were almost like Rority's pets.

"Yeah, she has to go herself on that one," Gumal said. "I turned that one down, too. This is nothing like that. All I have to do is retrieve a device we planted about fifty thousand BB. We're supposed to pick it up in 10 AB."

"What's the device for? Why do we let it sit so long?"

"It's an ancient time device, sent back from millions of years ago when we were still experimenting and learning how to break the spacetime barrier. It was supposed to send back data, but never did. It sat there for fifty thousand years before I went and got it. Want to go along?" he asked again.

"Nah, I'm busy studying subatomic biochemistry," he said, grinning. Gumal snickered. Rority laughed. Gumal laughed harder. "Whoo!" Gumal exclaimed. "Good thing we weren't drinking and stratodoobing!"

Now, I can no more understand the humans than an Australopithecus could have understood us protohumans, let alone describe them well. I certainly can't understand their humor, it just seems dumb to me. They were laughing about the fact that Rority had been reading a scholarly paper on some aspect of biochemistry that was written some time in the middle of the first century AB, with the primitive date 2005, that they thought was hilarious.

They think we're funny. Of course, I'm amused when someone gets too close to the chimpanzee cage and gets feces thrown at him.

Monkeys are funny.

A Guinness floated into Rority's hand. “Want a beer?” he asked.

“Sure. Where's your stratodoober?”

“I don't know, but it'll be in your hand in a minute” he said as Gumal plucked the beer from the air, and its nobotic transport crumbled to microscopic dust and the stratodoober floated toward him from wherever it had been.

“So why did we let this ancient probe sit so long? Why do they want it back, anthropology?” Rority asked.

“No, it leaked gravitational waves,” Gumal said. “It sat there for tens of thousands of years leaking before I went back and got it. Fortunately they were high frequency waves, making them pretty much non-omnidirectional, with a pretty tight beam. It only had effects for a few hundred kilometers, and got weaker on a logarithmic scale as you got further from the probe's beam. The probe itself is about a kilometer or two underwater.”

“Effects?” Rority asked.

“The effects? They went away a couple hundred years after I got it. There were strange optical anomalies that stretched to the edges of the beam's effect. Sometimes in that region, even at the very edges, the water looked like sky and the sky looked like ocean. Closer in and electronic devices and mechanical compasses malfunctioned and failed.

“Things that went through the beam's center were displaced in time; the closer to the center, the further in spacetime they went. A squadron of ancient protohuman warplanes crashed thousands of years after the device was first planted because of the time distortion, but they didn't see the significance at first because it was believed that if anything was displaced in time, it wouldn't be where the Earth was when the effect was completed. It turns out they were wrong.

“It led to incredible advances in mathematics and gravitron theory way back then, which led to pretty much everything that followed. The new maths also showed that had we not sent the probe, those new maths would never have been discovered except by an incredibly improbable set of coincidences or a really weird person, which I guess would also be an incredibly improbable coincidence.

“Of course, the existence of life itself was caused by an incredibly improbable set of coincidences. We're lucky to find any kind of life at all in one out of a hundred galaxies. It's extremely rare, and is just an incredibly unlikely feature of entropy.

“It didn't affect anything but ocean creatures and the occasional boaters until about three or four hundred BB when the protohumans started shipping and traveling across what was then known as the Atlantic. After that, of course, legends started when ships, and later aircraft, were lost in the region. Most of the legends were hokum, but a few were pretty close to what really happened.”

He took another toke off the stratodoober and another sip of his beer.

Rority said “I would have thought that the ancient protohumans would have found it when they sent space probes up studying gravitational waves.”

“The beam was never pointed anywhere near one of the satellites,” replied Gumal. “Besides, I retrieved it before they launched them. If one of the probes had experienced the effects they'd have thought it was simply defective.”

Rority said “Sounds like an interesting assignment.”

“The interesting part's done; that was reading the report. The picking up the device is nothing. Want me to get some beer when I'm there?”

“Sure, and look Albert up and tell him... Oh hell, I'll go along.”

“Thanks, it's less boring when you have company.”

Chapter 24

Earthian War

"Lieutenant Maris reporting as ordered, sir."

"Sit down, Maris. Coffee? Cigar?" Colonel Gorn offered.

"Cigar, sir?" Maris asked, puzzled. Gorn laughed.

"Private O'Brien gave it to me," he said. "His wife's pregnant and he's been giving cigars away to everybody. I'm happy for the young man, but I don't have any use for a cigar."

"Well, thank you sir, but neither do I, and he already gave me one anyway."

Maris waited respectfully for Gorn to get to the damned point.

He didn't.

"Lucky kids, those O'Briens," the Colonel said. "Not many babies getting born these days."

"No, sir. There aren't. The O'Briens are indeed lucky."

"Yep, damned few babies."

"Yes, sir. Damned few."

"I'm curious, Maris," said Gorn, finally getting to the damned point, to Maris' great relief. "You must be some kind of a genius."

"Sir?" asked Maris.

"The way you knew the Venusians were going to Saturn as soon as the first rocket lifted off. It's almost like you can read their minds," Gorn said, giving Maris a suspicious look and thinking of Picard.

"Oh," said Maris, "That was easy, just simple math."

"Simple math?"

"Yes, sir. I calculated their trajectories and there was no way they would wind up here. Either all their mathematicians are idiots like Zales thinks, or they were going someplace else for some other reason. And as close as they were going to the sun it suggested a slingshot.

"Jupiter and Neptune are on this side of the sun right now, so the only place they could possibly be going would be Saturn. It and Venus are the only planets on that side of the sun right now. The only reason I could think of why they'd be going there is to go to war with the Titanians, but I can't for the life of me figure out why, though."

"Maris," replied Gorn, "You *are* a fucking genius." He laughed. "No, you're just a genius, you and O'Brien together make a fucking genius," he said, holding the cigar.

"But seriously, Maris, I'm impressed. That was good work, and it's going to look very good on your record."

"Well, thank you, sir," said Maris, "it's good to know that one is appreciated."

"You are, Lieutenant. Very well done! Dismissed."

"Yes, sir," said Maris, rising from his chair. "Thank you, sir," he said again, saluting.

The colonel returned his salute, and Maris sauntered down to the workshop where Johnson and O'Brien were tending the screens.

"Anything going on, men?" he asked.

"Not much, sir," said O'Brien. "Washington's slaughtering barflies, Ford's sleeping, and they're trying to take out satellites."

"Are they having much luck?"

"No, sir. They sent up thirty rockets and the satellites destroyed them all. Washington hasn't got laid yet, either."

"Is that germane, Private?" Maris said, suppressing a grin.

"Why, yes sir, it is," O'Brien replied. "He's not nearly as disgusting once he gets his teensy little pecker wet. He usually just staggers back to his palace and passes out and we have a nice, peaceful night. Except maybe for the occasional rocket base commander committing suicide."

Maris chuckled. "Good point, Private."

"Excuse me, Lieutenant, sir," said Johnson. "Larry, he's going to another rocket facility."

"After bar hopping?" O'Brien said, incredulous. "That's not normal for him. Shit! Greg, did he get laid tonight? Did you listen to everything he had to say?"

"Yeah, he got laid, and I think I heard everything, at least until the Lieutenant came in," Johnson replied. He looked at the Lieutenant. "Sorry, sir," he said.

"No problem, Johnson. I take it you'll watch the recording, O'Brien?"

"Yes sir, of course. That's standard procedure."

"OK, I'll get out of you guys' way and let you do your jobs. Keep me posted."

"Yes, sir," said O'Brien, turning to his screens. He put the video back by two minutes."

"Hark!" said Colonel Sharpley, saluting.

"At ease, Colonel. How fast can you get a two thousand man ship ready?"

"Immediately, sir, within the hour."

"Excellent," said Washington. "Man your ship and make it ready for liftoff in two hours."

"Yes sir. What is our destination and further orders?"

"You're to go to Earth and start construction of a military base at the planetary coordinates in this packet," he said, handing a packet to the new Earth base's commander. "We're colonizing Earth one month after we've destroyed Mars."

"Sir?" Queried the Colonel. "Destroy Mars? With all due respect, sir, and in fact all respect period, but we can destroy Mars?"

"That's classified, Colonel. Just get that rocket to Earth. Dismissed."

"Yes, sir," said the Colonel, saluting. Washington left.

"Bloody hell," said O'Brien. "Watch my screens, Greg, I have to go talk to Maris."

O'Brien walked down the hall to the Lieutenant's office and knocked on the door. “Come,” ordered Maris.

“Sir, the Venusians are launching a warship towards Earth, where they plan to set up a base. Washington seems to have a plan to destroy Mars.”

Maris picked up an instrument and spoke to it. “EL2, there is a Venusian warship headed for Earth. Stop it with any means necessary. Reply when you get this message.”

It would be a few minutes before the radio waves reached the troops stationed at Earth's L2 Lagrange point. He spoke again.

“Colonel Gorn, please,” he said, and laid the instrument down.

“Be glad you're not an officer, private,” he said to O'Brien.

“Yes sir. The shit really seems to have hit the fan, sir. Am I dismissed? I should be watching the screens, all that's on duty right now is Johnson and me and he's still pretty green.”

“Yes, O'Brien, you're right, dismissed. Damn.”

Maris' device beeped. O'Brien saluted and left.

“Gorn here,” said the device. “What's the problem, Lieutenant?”

“Venus is attempting to establish a base on Earth, sir. Rather than shoot it down from a satellite I've alerted EL2 instead. The Venusians won't know what happened to it that way and won't miss it for a while. If we kill it from a satellite they'll just launch another one.

“The Venusians are sure they can destroy Mars as well. Maybe they've contacted the Titanians? Maybe they're not attacking them but teaming up with them? Or trying to steal technology from them? We don't really know anything about the Titanians.”

“This is mere speculation, Maris.”

“Yes, sir, it is. Merely a hypothesis with no way to test it. But it worries me, sir. They seem to be certain they can destroy us.”

"Well, thank you, Lieutenant. Keep me posted. Dismissed."

"Yes sir," said Maris, who "hung up" the "phone".

Gorn was worried; Maris had a knack for seeing what most people missed, the rockets going to Saturn instead of Mars being a very good example. He was glad he had a man like Maris, but now he had to worry about the Titanians as well as the Venusians.

What could they possibly be up to? What in the galaxy could the Venusians hope to gain by going to Saturn?

Two weeks later as the Venusian battleship thundered silently through the vacuum of space towards the Earth, ten automated rockets streaked towards it from Earth's L2 Lagrange point, also thundering silently because in space, no one can hear you thunder.

There was a tense atmosphere on board the Venusian battleship.

"Captain, I thought I picked something up dead ahead, but it only flickered for a second."

"Are you sure, Commander?"

"No sir, I... oh, no, this is bad. Sir, I think there's a missile headed towards us!"

The captain closed a contact and gave terse orders. "All hands, red alert! Evasive action. Battle stations! Brace for impact!"

Those were his last words, as a second later ten hydrogen bombs from ten automated rockets that had been launched from Earth's L2 Lagrange point unleashed atomic hell on the warship.

The blasts didn't even leave any debris.

Chapter 25

The Zeta Reticuli Incident

"Wow!" said Betty. "Did you see that?"

"See what?" Barney asked.

"A shooting star. Only it's shooting *upward*. And it looks like it's getting closer. Stop the car so we can get a better look. Besides, I think the dog needs to pee."

"Give me a second, Betty, there are bears around here. Let me get my gun." He got the pistol and binoculars from the Chevy's trunk and handed a pair of the binoculars to Betty.

She said "It's... that's really funny looking. It went across the moon and it looked weird." Both were looking through their binoculars at the sky, presumably no longer very worried about the bears.

"Airplane?" Barney surmised.

"Maybe it's a flying saucer," Betty said. "My sister saw a UFO a few years ago." Barney looked at it again. "That's no airplane! Lets get back in the car."

They drove slowly for a while. "Look! It's right over the Old Man of the Mountain! It's twice as big and looks like it's rotating."

It seemed that the object was playing cat and mouse with them, then headed straight for them, head-on. Barney slammed on the brakes.

It was maybe a hundred feet above the hills, and was *huge*. Barney got his gun from his pocket and stepped out of the car. A voice said "stay where you are and keep looking." Red lights on what appeared to be bat-wing fins began to telescope out of the sides of the craft, and a long structure descended from the bottom.

He saw about a dozen weird looking, almost humanoid figures in a window through his binoculars, all but one moving away from the window. Barney panicked and ran back to the car.

"They're going to capture us!" he screamed, jumping back in the car and peeling out as fast as he could.

Betty rolled the window of their '57 Chevy down and looked out – the stars had disappeared.

Beeping or buzzing sounds seemed to bounce off the trunk of the car. It vibrated, and a tingling sensation passed through the Hills' bodies. Betty touched the metal on the passenger door, expecting to feel an electric shock, but felt only the vibration. They felt weird, their minds felt dulled.

A second series of code-like beeping or buzzing sounds returned the couple to full consciousness. They found that they had traveled nearly thirty five miles south but had only vague, spotty memories of this section of road. They recalled making a sudden unplanned turn, encountering a roadblock, and observing a fiery orb in the road.

"That was pretty cool, Rula," said Rority. "I'm glad you talked us into coming. I thought you were really going to dissect them! Too bad they were so shook up about it, but I guess the samples were necessary."

"Well," Rula replied, "The samples are important, but it wasn't just the samples. This was documented. It had to happen, so it happened. I'm getting pretty good at math!" she said.

She looked at Rority sternly when she saw the relieved look on his face. "What, did you think I was going to cut his balls off, Rority? If the biologists are satisfied with the protohuman DNA we sampled, we won't need to do this again."

She added "We weren't going to dissect them, but we're going to butcher a cow before we go back to the present. And the samples from the protohumans look good."

"What about the nobots that were all over the car?" Gumal asked. "Won't they be a problem?"

"They're dead; they were programmed to shut themselves off after we left and they had revived the protohumans. Who in 16 AB could program nobots? Nobody could turn them back on back then."

Barney never could figure out why there were shiny concentric circles on the Bel Aire's trunk, or why if you put a compass near them, its needle spun.

"OK," said Rority, "go over to Ireland before we go back. I want to pick up a few cases of beer."

"Sure," said Rula, "But then we're going dancing."

Gumal groaned, and the friends he had invited along grumbled as well. "Damn, Rula, if we knew you were going dancing we wouldn't have come!" he said.

"Well, you guys were going to Zeta Reticuli, weren't you?" Rula said. "It really is really nice in this timeframe, and will be until the supernova ruins the pretty scenery in that part of the galaxy.

"All the college kids go on Spring break there now and I hear it's pretty wild, you'll have a blast. I'd go along if I hadn't planned the dance lessons. Just pick us up on your way back.

"Did you bring your stratodoober, Rority? I want a hit!"

Chapter 26

Martian Catastrophe

Sargent Zales was awakened in the small hours of the morning by an obnoxiously loud communications device. Maris was on the talker when he answered. "Zales here, What's up, sir?"

"Get down to the base ASAP, Sargent. Mars is under attack! Call your men."

"Under attack? Holy shit, Lieutenant! I mean, uh, yes sir. I'll be right there, sir." Zales disconnected and called his men before waking his wife.

"Honey? Wake up! I have to go to the base, we're on alert. Lieutenant Maris just called and said Mars is under attack!"

"Hmmmphft... whah... WHAT? Mars is under attack? Who's attacking us, Venusians?"

"I guess, I don't know any more than you, all he said was that we're under attack and I have to get there ASAP. Holy shit! Mars hasn't been at war for a hundred years! Where's my pants, honey? Holy shit!"

Back on the base, Lieutenant Maris was debriefing Private O'Brien.

"No sir," O'Brien said, "none of the Venusian rockets went south. They were slightly north of the planetary plane, less than a percent, and they looked like they were going towards Saturn. If I may ask, sir, what's going on?"

Maris was grave. "Brace yourself, Private. Everybody in the southern hemisphere of Mars appears to be dead. We've found no survivors. There was massive ionizing radiation, we don't know the cause."

O'Brien went pale, even paler than was usual with the pasty-skinned Martians – most of his family lived in the southern hemisphere. And a lot of his friends lived there, too. Military command was in the southern hemisphere as well, and Colonel Gorn was probably now in charge of Mars' remaining military. Thank Deimos the civilian government was in the north!

"Blimey," O'Brien thought, even though there hadn't been anything resembling an Englishman or an Irishman for millions of years and they speak a completely different language ten million years in our future.

"Sir? ...everybody?" A tear left O'Brien's eye, and he blushed, trembling.

"Private, you can mourn later. Right now we need you, and badly. Those screens could mean Mars' survival. The entire south was flooded with gamma rays and we need to make sure the north doesn't get hit too."

"Y-yes sir," he stammered. "Galaxy!" he said. Everybody dead? It was beyond his comprehension. He put his focus on the screens.

"And Private," Maris continued, "it may have been a natural phenomenon. We don't know the cause yet."

A while later, Zales showed up. "O'Brien!" he said, "Did the lieutenant tell you..."

"Yeah, Sarge, he was here a little while ago."

"Have you called Dennis?"

"No, I've been too busy manning these screens."

"Call her, I'll take over. Fucking shit, I can't believe this is happening!"

O'Brien's wife was watching a newscast and went paler than normal for a Martian when the talker signaled. A commercial message was playing on the screen as the device signaled. "Pist," the screen said. "An affordable levitator that will work in any floater! Remember, Pist means quality! Get the original! Get Pist!"

The Pist jingle followed.

"Larry?" she said as the commercial played its Pist jingle. "What's wrong? What's happened?"

"Oh honey," he sobbed. "They're all dead!"

"Who's dead? Larry..."

"Oh, Galaxy, Dennis, *everybody!* The Venusians came up with some sort of gamma ray weapon that murdered everyone on the south side of the planet. They're all dead! Everyone! My family..."

"We interrupt this newscast for some breaking news," the newscast interrupted after the commercial break was over, of course not interrupting the commercial.

"Everybody? Larry..."

O'Brien sobbed. "As far as we can tell. Look, honey, I wish I could come home but we need to make sure they can't hit this hemisphere too," he said, tears streaming down his face. "Damn those murderous ghouls! Galaxy, but I hope Hoo decides to nuke 'em once and for all."

"Oh dear, oh dear, oh dear," Dennis said. "Look, Larry, I'll make lunch for you guys and bring it there. Oh, my..."

O'Brien went back to his screens, wiping tears from his face. It was too horrible to contemplate. If they hit the north, too...

Chapter 27

Everything You Know Is Wrong

"I don't know what this is going to mean," Gumal said, "but Rula told me the number guys say something's terribly wrong. As wrong as two plus two equaling five and having it be the correct answer. Something to do with reality not agreeing with itself. Rounding errors showing up in the real world, where there should be no such thing as a rounding error."

Rority laughed. "You mean like going back in time and shooting your grandfather before your father was conceived?" He laughed even louder.

"No, seriously, that's exactly... well, not *exactly* it, but close. Things that happened didn't, and things that didn't, did. Like, their maths say that I don't mind being nobotically manipulated into a protohuman."

"But 'paradoxes', as the ancients called them, don't exist in the real universe," said Rority. "They can't. No matter how hard you tried, even if you could go back that short of time without the feedback destroying your ship, no matter how hard you tried you couldn't kill him. It's a law of physics."

"Not being able to go faster than light was once a law of physics," Gumal answered.

"Yes, but the protohuman Einstein got his math right, it was just that we discovered ways around the roadblocks." His beer hit the ground with a crash and he sat there like a stone, not even breathing.

"Rority? Are you OK?" Gumal said. He got up and walked over and lifted Rority's hand - which came off in a shower of nobotic dust before disintegrating, along with the rest of Rority.

"Shit!" Gumal exclaimed. "Rority's a nobotic robot! News!" he ordered, and a "book" appeared in his hand, risen from Rority's ashes.

The headline screamed "supernova wipes out almost all life in southern hemisphere." Gumal swore again and read on, not thinking of the conversation he'd been having with the apparently now-deceased Rority, only how much he was going to miss his partner and best friend.

Then he realized where he was – he was visiting Rority at Rority's place. Why was there a robot impersonator? And why did it stop? He called Ragwel, a nobot programmer he often drank and stratodoobed with, and one of those he had taken to that wild party on Zeta Reticuli.

Rority's Guinness hit the floor with a crash. "What the... Gumal! I can't see!" he said excitedly.

Gumal didn't answer.

"Gumal? Where are you?"

As bad as going blind is to those of us protohumans who are unfortunate enough to lose our eyesight, it's even worse for humans ten million years in our future. Humans don't get sick; not any kind of sick. The nobots repair any damage to any cell before it has a chance to cause real harm, so going blind is unthinkable for a human.

For the first time in his life... indeed, the first time in anybody's lives for millions of years, Rority was scared. Not just scared, but terrified. He got up cautiously, and it seemed his chair felt different than it did when he could see. He stretched his arms out in front of him and groped in the direction Gumal had been sitting. Gravity seemed weird and he almost stumbled. He took another two steps – and hit a solid surface.

Well, almost solid. It felt kind of like cloth, sort of soft. He heard what almost sounded like muffled screams on the other side of the barrier. He pushed harder and the obstacle gave way. "Gumal?" he yelled through the hole he had torn.

"W-who's there?" a shaky voice said in the darkness. And... it seemed to Rority that it wasn't quite as dark now. There was a tiny bit of greenish light that he could almost see by.

He almost saw that he was in a sort of cube, maybe five meters to a side, and he could almost see that there was a hole in it where he'd pushed through. Almost.

Just almost, he thought, anyway. He wasn't yet sure if he could really see anything or not.

"It's Rority, is that you, Gumal? I can't see!"

"No, my name's Gromwel. I don't know any Gumal. I can't see, either. You say your name's Rority?"

"Yeah," he replied. "I was sitting here at home drinking a beer with my partner Gumal and everything went black."

"Same here, I was playing Babel with my friend Ornda and it went black and she's gone!"

"What in the spacetime continuum could have happened?"

"I don't know, but I think the nobots stopped working. Do you know any good programmers?"

Rority said "Dunno, maybe programmers wouldn't be any help. The nobots seem to be completely gone. And so is the world."

"The world's not gone, but I don't know where we are. I was outside and now apparently I'm not. And I think I can see now... a little... but it seems really dark in here, wherever 'here' is."

They both started tearing at the fabric, which sparked faintly with every tear. An hour later they'd discovered a dozen other people in similar cubes. One of them was an expert in nobotics, who said his name was Noob.

"I'd think it was an EMP that did this," Noob said, "but how in the hell could an EMP blast through all of this? At any rate I don't have the tools I need to research it. It also appears that they didn't teach me everything about nobots, and I hold a PhD!"

Gromwel snickered. “Everybody holds a PhD!”

“Yes,” Noob said, “but mine is in nobotics. What's your field?”

"I'm an Ornitholinguist”

"Really? You study the language of birds?”

"Yep. Not much use in this situation, is it? What should we do? The air doesn't seem to be getting thinner, and there's a tiny bit of light. Should we look for more people?”

“I can only talk a second,” Ragwel said. “Really busy. Half the nobots on the planet are dead, and we're starting to learn that reality isn't real.”

“Huh?” Gumal asked, puzzled. “Isn't that the math boys' domain?”

“No, that's not what I meant,” Ragwel said. “I mean that you're not where you think you are. The supernova unearthed evidence that millions of years ago we stopped face to face communications and all live in nobot fantasies that are actually just cubes containing us. Nothing you've ever done in your life is real. Nothing. It's all a farce!”

“So, what do we do?”

“Now? Study. Live nobots are already rebuilding the matrix on the southern hemisphere and we hope that even though the electromagnetic pulse from the nova knocked the nobots out, maybe the nobots themselves were enough of a shield to keep radiation harmful to us out.

“The nobots could have produced the same radiation out of phase and canceled most of it out with destructive interference, but it would have overloaded every one of their circuits and burned them all out.

“Now I have to go, I need to get trillions of nobots to the other hemisphere so if there are survivors they'll have food, drink, and medical attention for the radiation poisoning they may have suffered; some radiation must have gotten through, considering the power of that blast.

“Also, the nobots are going to need to work on the atmosphere – the planet's ozone shield is gone and the atmosphere is polluted with oxides of nitrogen. Nobody's written a program that will fix it, yet anyway. I may have to.”

“Wait! How do I get out of the fantasy? What do you mean by ‘matrix’?”

“It's a matrix of cubes made from nobots. Getting out is what we're working on now. I'll call.”

Chapter 28

This is your Farmer on Drugs

"Whoa, mule! What's wrong with you?" McGregor said sternly. His mule had been more and more restless for half an hour now; probably spooked by all the dogs barking, he thought. Now a wind was blowing and the air had a nasty smell.

Reverend Smith was walking down the lane toward McGregor's farm, and started feeling light-headed. The air smelled funny, he thought. The trees seemed scared – this was strange. Scared trees? But the way they were moving sure looked like they were scared.

McGregor, seeing that no work was going to be done this morning thanks to that finicky, stubborn mule, unhitched it from the plow and started walking it towards the barn, leaving the plow in the field for tomorrow.

His head felt kind of weirdly strange a little as he unbridled the mule, and he started staggering. Everything looked funny; he rubbed his eyes and saw Smith staggering towards him. He giggled; Reverend Smith staggering?

"Are you OK, John?" McGregor said. "You look a little unsteady."

Smith giggled. "You don't look so steady yourself." They both started laughing uproariously.

"I don't know what's so funny," McGregor said, and laughed again.

"Those cows are funny!" Smith said, giggling.

"Hey! My cattle!" McGregor exclaimed excitedly. "What's wrong with them?" The cattle were all spooked, terrified.

"Oh, Lord," laughed the intoxicated preacher. "Look at that funny tree! It's sinking!" He started laughing again at the leaning, sinking tree. "That's hilarious!"

"Sinkhole!" McGregor yelled, and started running to the cattle pen's gate before falling down. He got up and continued to the gate, this time at a quick stagger. Smith sat down on the ground, his head spinning.

McGregor opened the gate, but he was too late for half his cattle, who had fallen into the ever-widening hole. It was certainly a sobering experience, even though he still fell down and laid there for a few minutes after opening the gate, not the least bit sober.

"Reverend!" he cried, when he started regaining his senses and saw the preacher laying prostrate on the ground. He felt like his head was clearing somewhat. A little.

Maybe.

Neither the farmers, nor anyone else yet, could have any idea that a supernova had obliterated the Acrux star system three hundred twenty one years earlier, and that the gamma rays from the supernova had just arrived at the solar system at the speed of light, killing everything on the southern half of all the system's planets and burning much of Sol's planets' nitrogen into many different and varied oxides.

Their ozone layers were gone, too, thanks to the chemistry caused by the combustion and the various chemicals that were released and mixed by it. It was the same on all the terraformed solar planets as well, and most likely other stellar systems also suffered the same fates.

Something similar, except it wasn't really, had happened more than once. An example was an exploding star that had affected the Earth four hundred fifty million years earlier, causing a mass extinction called the Ordovician event. This is only one of the many examples available.

What usually caused these mass extinctions on Earth was some angry, petulant, unsociable, mean-tempered, obnoxious, fatassed little superstar who couldn't hold his mass and finally blew up under the pressure.

This was not an angry, petulant, unsociable, mean-tempered, obnoxious, fat little superstar blowing up under pressure.

This supernova was man-made. And it was an accident.

Well, it was sort of an accident. Like World War One on Earth was started. Sort of an accident.

Or just maybe bad planning. But it doesn't matter, they had been dead for over three hundred years, and were not going to face the consequences of their actions, since they already had faced them over three hundred years earlier and were long dead.

Planets around stars that are near, cosmically speaking, these phenomena are greatly affected by them. On Earth-type planets, with mostly nitrogen atmospheres, much of the nitrogen combusted. The combustion produced various nitrogen oxides, mostly what protohumans who used hydrocarbons for fuel had called "smog,"

The oxide affecting McGregor's farm was what is commonly known to us as nitrous oxide. It had taken days to travel there from the southern hemisphere, and the oxides that reached them were at least improbable. But reach them they did.

"Laughing gas" is what nitrous oxide is usually known as.

"Reverend? Wake up! Are you OK? Oh, Yeshuah..."

The preacher's eyes fluttered open. "What happened?" he asked.

"A sinkhole in my cattle pen," McGregor answered. "Whoa... look inside that hole!"

What appeared to be steam or smoke was wafting out.

"I think you might want to call a meeting, Reverend."

"Yes, I think you're... Oh, Lord! Devils! Watch and pray, I'll get help. You might want to get your pitchfork."

McGregor stared at the hole in horror as the reverend ran away.

Chapter 29

The Venusian Triumph

"You dare to awaken me, stooge?" Washington said, pulling out his fryer and aiming it at the hapless youngster who had been ordered to his death by his more sensible superiors, who would much rather he die than they.

"I'm really really *really* sorry, General sir, your highness," the cadet said, shaking and sweating, "but I was ordered... *ordered, sir!* To wake you and inform your worshipful majesty that the Martians have struck the first volley in the war. Everyone in the Southern hemisphere is dead!" he exclaimed, trembling, his eyed closed tightly.

The General smiled happily. "It's OK, cadet, I'm not going to kill you." He adjusted a control on his microwave pistol and fired at the cadet, who fell to the floor screaming in agony from third degree burns.

"I'll bet you're wishing I'd killed you about now," Washington said, chuckling. He ordered that the cadet be moved to the infirmary and promoted and that Ford be awakened and summoned. Ford showed up quickly.

"Hark!" he said, saluting as he entered.

"Shut up, Ford," Washington said, "it's just us. You can set the formalities aside. I have some great news! Those foolish chalkies have done Venus a wonderful favor!

"Actually many favors! They've irradiated the entire southern half of the planet and killed everyone for us. Plus, we no longer need to cook up an excuse to exterminate them."

"Exterminate them? But how, sir?" Ford asked incredulously. "If they have some kind of super microwave blaster that can kill half a planet..."

“It's already in motion, Ford. I came up with a plan months ago. Since we knew spies had infiltrated us and planted bugs, I've been careful to not let any man know any more than a tiny piece, only as much as he needed. Only I know the plan. Even the captains of the warships are in the dark. Each has a set of orders that he is to open, read, and carry out at the appropriate time.”

“What's the plan?” asked Ford.

“It's too soon and I don't want it thwarted. Set up a press conference. I'm making a formal declaration of war against the Martians and telling our fellow Venusians how they attacked us.”

“Yes sir,” he said, saluting.

“Knock it off, Ford. Get that conference going.

“Yes sir,” Ford replied, and left.

Chapter 30

The Surface

Farmer Muldoon, whose leg had healed quickly after being nearly amputated by his plow, finished his plowing and started walking to the house. He was still limping slightly, holding the mule's bridle in his hand as he walked.

His wife was just finishing dinner preparations as he washed the field's grime off of himself, muscles aching in a good way and his injured leg aching in a not so good way. He'd gotten a lot done but was feeling a little ill, and his head was swimming. The air smelled funny, too.

There was a beautiful sunset as the Muldoons sat on the porch after they had eaten, enjoying the beauty God had given them and drinking the communion wine and munching the communion bread and watching the lightning bugs just starting to blink, and laughing for no apparent reason at all.

Dried leaves were playing tag in the whirlwinds, apparently enjoying themselves almost as much as the Muldoons were.

Reverend Smith pulled up in his buggy a while after Jonah had pointed out the beautiful Evening Star to Rebekkah as the sun sat just under the trees. The reverend's horse was panting and sweating as if he'd been run too hard and too long.

"Well, hello, John!" Jonah said lightheartedly. "What brings you out here this fine evening? You look troubled."

"I am, Jonah, I am. We have serious trouble; serious bad trouble. Terrible trouble. Some devils have escaped from hell and have tunneled their way up here! Get your pitchforks, we may have a fight."

"Pitchforks? Fight? John, are you ill?"

Jonah was worried; the reverend was more devoted to Yeshua than any man he'd ever known. He was not the sort of man to commit any violence at all, and in fact just a month earlier a drunken young man had punched him so hard it had knocked the preacher to the ground.

Rather than striking back in anger as Jonah feared he might have done had he been in the same situation, the pastor had gotten up, dusted himself off, and offered to let the youth hit him again!

The young man had started shaking, and fell to his knees, sobbing and begging forgiveness, and the holy man had forgiven him.

Now here was the Reverend Smith, all wild-eyed and screaming for blood. Had he gone mad? Was he possessed by a devil? Maybe one of the devils he had been spouting off about?

"Reverend," said Jonah, "I don't understand. God Himself guards hell. Perhaps He's testing you?"

"You must come with me!" screamed the distraught preacher. "Please! Jonah, I'm begging you! *Please!!*"

"You go ahead and help the reverend," Rebekkah said, patting Jonah on the arm. "He's mighty upset and God only knows what he's capable of in his state of mind. I'll stay here and pray."

Jonah kissed her on the forehead, told her he loved her, got a pitchfork and left with the preacher.

The Muldoons nor any of the other of the other Amish knew that the entire southern hemisphere was dead. Nor did they know that humans had survived the apocalypse in the self-made prison that they had just discovered.

Nor did they even know that these humans even existed.

The Amish were more like protohumans than true humans; human evolution had been self-directed, while the Amish thought technology was evil and had shunned it since times long forgotten. Species only evolve when their environment changes, and unknown to them, the nobots had kept the Earth's surface in nearly perfect harmony. Life had changed very little in millions of years on the planet's surface.

They also didn't know that they had been known as "controls" when humans had started living in their nobot-constructed fantasies, fantasies that until now they thought were real.

But the underground humans had still striven to learn, and there were still people capable of programming nobots, and even getting information out of the trillions of trillions of trillions of trillions of bits of data the nobots held. Their research, triggered by the destruction of half the nobots on Earth, uncovered the fact that they had been underground for millions of years and living mostly fantasies.

The rounding errors were understood now. Reality has no rounding errors, but digital devices do. It's especially pronounced when they're all networked together and half of them stop working all at once.

They had reprogrammed the matrix of cubes in a small section to slowly collapse, and a sinkhole had opened in McGregor's pasture and swallowed half his cattle. He was standing by the large hole when Smith and Muldoon arrived.

Rority had opted to actually travel, which he hadn't known he'd never really done, to the northern hemisphere to visit his partner, who he hadn't known he'd never really seen, until the catastrophe pulled the wool off of everyone's eyes.

He and Gumal, probably the world's best known of anthropologists, archeologists, and protohistorians were chosen to investigate life on the surface.

Life on the surface was holding crude weapons with pointed tines. "Garbouok are grato! Gutably!" one of them babbled.

"Protohumans? Now?" Rority thought.

"Oh shit," Gumal thought.

Smith saw them and pointed McGregor's spare pitchfork at them. "Back to hell, devils! In Yeshua's name I command you!" he ordered.

Muldoon now understood what Reverend Smith had meant; this had been prophesied. The antichrist had come, followed by Christ, and Satan had been banished to hell, but the prophesies said he'd be back in a thousand years.

In actuality it had been more than a few million.

"Uh, I don't like the looks of this," Gumal said.

"They're speaking in tongues, Reverend," Jonah said.

"No," replied the preacher, "tongues is the language of God, anyone can understand Him. These devils simply speak a different language than us, and one that seems clearly evil to me."

"I can't understand them," Gumal said. Rority held his hand out and a small rod appeared.

"Back to hell, devils! In Yeshua's name I command you!" the rod said out loud.

"They're speaking in tongues, Reverend," the rod continued. "No," it replied to itself, "tongues is the language of God, anyone can understand Him. These devils simply speak a different language, and one that seems clearly evil to me."

"Shit!" exclaimed Gumal. "We're going about this the wrong way."

"Agreed," said Rority. "Lets go back down and figure out how to solve this. Nobots! Make it look to these creatures that everything is as it was!"

Smith, McGregor, and Muldoon stared in amazement as the swallowed cattle came back to the surface and the ground filled itself in and the vegetation that had been growing seemed to have never been disrupted.

All of them wondered if it had been a hallucination, since they had all felt so strange earlier, but none would ever wonder out loud if they had indeed been hallucinating.

"Thank you, Lord," the preacher said to the sky, "for showing us this miracle. Help us to understand it! Amen."

The other two echoed "Amen."

"Well," Gumal said to Rority, "we really fucked that one up."

"Amen to that," Rority said. "Now what?"

Chapter 31

Morlocks

"Well, crap," Rority said. "I guess we're Morlocks."

Noob was puzzled. "We're what?"

"Morlocks," Rority replied. "It's from an ancient book by a protohuman named H. G. Wells. This fellow's story has a man travel through time to the future, and finds a peaceful society named the Eloi. But of course, like most of the protohuman fiction, it turns ugly and the reader is introduced to another society, the Morlocks, who live underground and eat Eloi. It's no wonder these people are afraid of us!

"But at any rate, what have you found out about the nobots?" he asked.

"The data were hard to find," Noob said, "since they were so old. I can't pin a date on it, but a few million years ago after we'd started making everything out of nobots, we collectively decided to build the matrix of nobotic cubes that gave us our present paradise. I fear it may now end, but maybe it's for the best. We've made little scientific progress in a long time. We just had no need.

"But you're the anthropologists," the programmer said. "What should we do about the species living on the surface?"

"Gumal's the anthropologist, I'm just a prehistorian archaeologist. What do you think, Gumal?"

"I think I need a hell of a lot more data," Gumal said. "We know little about them."

"Odd that I should be teaching history to a historian," Noob said, "but we're both descended from a common ancestor. The people on the surface were originally known as 'Controls' because they didn't want to live in a fantasy world made out of nobotic cubes. They considered themselves in control of the situation.

“We, of course, were called ‘Experimentals’ because we were performing experiments. I still have quite a bit more research to do and data to uncover and collect, but there were groups of protohumans called ‘Amish’ who were against all technology. As I said, I haven't yet found very much of the data, but I suspect that the Controls; or Eloi, as your protobook calls them, are these Amish people.”

“Do they have beer?” Rority asked, smirking.

“I haven't found any references to beer, but it's quite possible since they were originally Germanic people. I'm surprised you don't know, since you're the archaeologist,” said Noob.

”I was joking,” said Rority. “Some of them did, but most of them abstained from any alcohol except wine, and then only during communion.”

“During what?” asked Gumal.

“One of their primitive rituals, it isn't important. I'm excited at the prospect of studying these people, to see how different they are from us and from protohumans. They seem more like protohumans than humans, with not much evolution at all except how goofy they look. Or would to a protohuman. It isn't all that surprising, since they would never accept genetic modifications, and the environment was tamed long before we entered our cubes.

“But Noob, what about the Martians and Venusians? Are they a fiction, like most of our lives have been up until now?”

“Oh, they're real, all right. We'd terraformed both planets before we buried ourselves and those data were all confirmed. There were certainly people living on those planets once, and there are probably still people there unless the supernova or something else killed them.

“Venus had a problem with carbon dioxide before it was terraformed, it's possible the greenhouse effect could have run wild again. We're just going to have to have someone visit them to see, unless somebody can think of a way of long distance communication. Most likely, sending nobots would be faster than trying out various radio frequencies until we found one they were listening to."

"So much to catch up on," Rority said. "I'll send some nobotic sentinels to gather data on the Eloi; artificial birds, rabbits, squirrels, insects, and so on."

Gumal took a toke of his stratodoober and wondered about the Eloi he'd referred to. "I hope they don't try to eat... oh, hell, what am I thinking? They can't hurt a nobotic robot!"

Two weeks later they assembled again, this time a larger group with Rula and a few other disciplines. "Well," said Rority, "no beer, damn it!"

Gumal said "what about strato DOH! Of course no stratodoobers, what am I thinking? They're against technology."

"Well, boys," said Rula, "what are your plans?"

"We're sending radio messages to Mars and should get a signal from the Venusian probe tomorrow, but Venus is behind the sun right now so it will be a few more days to see what's up with it," replied Akwort, the planetologist. "From our telescope signals it looks like the terraforming on Mars has held, but we don't yet know if people still survive. If we don't hear from Mars we'll send a probe there, too."

Turning to Gumal, Rula asked "What about these so-called 'Eloi' or 'Amish' or whatever they're called? Can we and should we reintegrate?"

"Impossible," he answered. "They think we're devils from hell. If we want to go up to the top it will have to be in the southern hemisphere. It's easy enough being invisible, but impossible to be one of them.

"I doubt it would still be possible to procreate with them, considering how long we've been separate from their species. We don't have any DNA samples from them yet, so we can't be sure, but I'm pretty certain it's unlikely. I mean would you want to have sex with one of them? Uhg!"

"Well, hell," she said. "And I wanted them to teach me some of their dances! Yes, Rority, I read your report. Did anybody bring their stratodoober?"

"I did," said Rority. "Anybody got any beer?"

Chapter 31

Crop Circles

"Uh, Sarge? You gotta see this!"

"See what, O'Brien?"

"We're getting radio signals from Earth! It's a really strange modulation pattern, but it's coming from Earth!"

"What? Are you sure it's coming from Earth? I can't believe the Earthians developed radio. I thought they had an anti-technological civilization? Move over, Private, let me look."

Sargent Zales had a good long look at O'Brien's screen, fiddled with a few controls, and was as surprised as the private was. "Hold down the fort, O'Brien, I think the Lieutenant should have a look at this."

"Sure thing, Sarge." O'Brien said. He was uneasy - first the entire southern hemisphere of Mars irradiated to lifelessness, and now these strange signals were coming from Earth. The signals were obviously artificial, but he couldn't decipher them.

"Galaxy be but this is weird," he said aloud to nobody in particular, because nobody in particular was there, Zales having gone to see Maris.

The Lieutenant was thinking that since Defense Command Headquarters was in the south, his own boss was now head of the entire remaining Martian military. He needed to recruit somehow, and promotions for the surviving troops were in order. He was to meet with Gorn later in the day to talk about the recruiting and promoting. He hadn't had time to see a newscast to find out what President Hoo had to say about the situation.

Meanwhile, the controls back on Earth had their own problems. They were holding a meeting in the church about some spooky, probably evilly demonic activity around their farms.

"You saw the circles, Reverend, what do you make of it?" Muldoon asked.

"Probably just kids... you know how teenagers are," Reverend Smith replied. "Remember the cows that got tipped over last year and you thought it was demonic, when it turned out that the kids next door were just doing a bit of old-fashioned cow tipping and confessed their sin?"

"But how would they make these circles?"

"I don't know," the Reverend replied, "but as long as nobody is harmed, I really don't think we need to worry about it. If it was just kids, they'll confess and repent. If it's evil we'll know soon enough."

"But this is scary, Reverend!" Muldoon said.

"Trust the Lord, Jonah. He knows what's best. Hasn't he always protected us? Where's your faith, man?"

Muldoon blushed. "You're right, of course, John. I'm being foolish."

A half kilometer beneath them held a different meeting.

"The Martians haven't answered," Rula said. "I think we should send a robotic probe to Mars and see if they're still there. The first probe is on its way to Venus now."

Gumal wondered about the circles their craft caused in the vegetation. "What about the controls? Won't this make them wonder?"

"Let 'em wonder," said Rula.

"Give me that stratodoober," said Rority.

"I ought to give it to the controls, those stiff necked assholes!" Gumal said.

On the other side of the sun, General Washington had blood in his eyes and death on his mind... and a happy heart, rare indeed for a Venusian. The deaths of billions on Venus' southern hemisphere, where the old leadership had been and where all the unrest came from, and the death of Mars if they were responsible. And they were.

Even if they weren't.

"But General, how could the Martians have developed the technology to do such a thing?" his second in command asked. "Even though they have far better technology and researchers than we do?

"That was a super weapon they loosed on us! They can kill half a planet! How could we fight anyone so powerful?" Ford was thinking that they should open communications with Mars and start peace talks, maybe even establish trade, but he knew Washington would kill him for even suggesting it.

"You forget, General Ford, that when we took over Venus we were far outmatched technologically by the previous regime. And I have a plan to wipe out the Martian menace once and for all, like I told you before."

"But sir, again... may I ask how?"

"We're going to throw rocks at them."

"Throw rocks at them, sir?"

"Yes, Ford, rocks. Big rocks. Mountain sized rocks. Extinction event sized rocks."

"Wow," Ford replied, "you're going to have to go an awful long way to find any rocks that big. After all, they used up almost the entire asteroid belt, plus Deimos and Phobos, plus every other big rock they could find this side of Saturn when they terraformed Mars. Almost all of the asteroid belt and a large part of Saturn's rings are already on Mars from their terraforming days."

"That and most of our carbon," Washington said. "The damned idiots that ran things before we took over gave it to them. But there are plenty of rocks still left around Saturn," Washington responded. "We have craft on the way already. It's a matter of Venus' survival!"

"Sir," general Ford said plaintively, "Don't you think we should make sure the Martians are behind it?"

"Certainly not. The populace is scared and angry and all riled up and we need a scapegoat, a visible enemy. People want revenge. So the Martians are responsible whether or not they're responsible.

"We're running out of room here on Venus," he added, "and we're taking Mars. We need it. And Earth afterward."

He apparently and very conveniently forgot that everyone in the southern hemisphere was dead. Washington wasn't content to own a single world, he wanted the entire solar system.

He was annoyed that the troops he'd sent to establish a base on the Earth seemed to have just vanished.

It was ironic that the Amish were worrying about the peaceful "devils" underground when the real threat was two hundred million kilometers away.

A week later, Rula had some bad news for everyone. "We received signals from Venus, and they were hard to decipher, but we did it. We have some big problems. It looks like they may be getting ready to wage war with Mars."

"Did we get signals from Mars?" Gumal asked.

"Yes, but they weren't aimed at us. They have spacecraft at Lagrange points and the signals were aimed at them. We don't know why they wouldn't answer us, but we think it may be that they're not as technologically developed as we are and simply can't understand us. We're trying again. We need to warn the Martians."

"Why?" asked Gumal. "We haven't had contact with them for at least a million years. They're surely a completely different species by now."

"Because of what we heard from intercepted Venusian signals. They plan to exterminate the Martians and take over Mars, and we'll surely be next. We need to contact the Martians and see if we can help. Venus is certainly not going to be friendly, but the Martians may be if we give them a reason to."

"Where's Rority?" Gumal asked.

"He's working with linguists to try and craft a message the Martians will understand. Meanwhile, we have probes around Venus, and we think the Venusians don't have the technology to detect them.

"You think things were dire when the supernova hit, it's going to get much worse. Gentlemen and ladies, it's interplanetary war and it's not going to be pretty."

Chapter 33

Venus and Mars

"Sarge? We've got more signals from Earth, and they're at least using a reasonable modulation. They seem to be words, but I can't read it. Want a look?"

"Sure, O'Brien," said Zales. The Sergeant sat down at the private's terminal and fiddled with its controls again as O'Brien frowned; he'd have to readjust his settings again. "Hmmm... nope, I can't make heads or tails of it, either. I'll take it to the Lieutenant."

Sgt. Zales was worried, but didn't show it to his underling. O'Brien was visibly worried, too, and neither knew why. Zales left to see Lieutenant Maris, who had a look at it.

"I can make out just a tiny little bit of this from a class I took in college, but not much. Sergeant, get the Colonel on the talker."

"Yes sir," said Zales. After speaking to the base commander's secretary on the phone he handed it to Maris.

"Sir," said the Lieutenant to the device, "we have a communication from Earth. No, sir, we can't read it, it seems to be in an archaic language. Uh, huh. Yes sir. Right away, sir."

He transmitted the undeciphered message to the Colonel, who transferred it to a historian, then contacted his civilian superior, Doctor Gump, Dean of the government physics department and in command of the military.

On Venus, General Washington was pleased with himself. "We launched Months ago, Ford. They should have reached Saturn, and two or three months from now the Martians will be gone."

"Is this necessary, General?" General Ford asked. "We have the entire southern hemisphere waiting for repopulation.

We don't need Mars now."

"Yes, we do, Ford," he snapped, annoyed at Ford's caution. "We need a scapegoat. The last thing we want is massive unrest. I've already addressed the Venusian populace and told them that the Martians were responsible and we were retaliating, and we'll wipe out the Martian menace once and for all."

"Nobody objected to exterminating the Martian people, as well as all the other species on Mars?"

"Of course not, any more than they minded wiping out the Vigers here. Why in the *galaxy* our ancestors would bring felines here I'll never understand. They should have realized what they'd evolve into no matter how tasty they are. At any rate, even if the Martians aren't a menace yet, they surely will be in time. They're a militaristic species. Now I don't want to hear any more about it. Do I make myself clear, Ford?"

"Yes sir, of course, General." General Ford didn't verbally loose his thoughts on Washington, or even roll his eyes of course, but he knew the Martians had never been aggressive until the Venusians had threatened them.

But Washington had bigger plans. He owned a planet now, but he wanted to own an entire solar system.

A Venusian solar system.

His solar system.

Back in the underground cube matrix on Earth, Rority was, of course, puffing his stratodoober and contemplating what Rula had told him. They had learned fairly quickly how to speak with the Martians and had even gotten face to face communications with them, hindered, of course, by the ten minute and lengthening time lag between planetary communications, since the Martians had no such things as timecievers.

The Martians were odd looking, Rula thought, odder than the controls, although not as strange as the evil-looking Venusians they had seen from intercepted signals from the Martian satellites circling Venus.

It made sense; Mars had been terraformed first, and the terraforming had taken millennia.

"Well," Rority thought, "time to go to Venus." Not in the flesh as he'd believed before the supernova had ripped aside the veil of artificial reality, but as an operator. It would seem the same; an operator was all he was before, even though he had previously been ignorant of the fact.

Ragwel was busy launching nobotic probes to intercept the Venusian warships, whose crews were certainly dead from the supernova's killing radiation.

Rula was busy planning the next stage. Intercepted communications from Venus showed that the Venusians were in the process of launching hundreds more rock interceptors, just in case. Of course, a good dictator was always prepared for anything, and always paranoid of everyone. He hadn't liked the look in Ford's eyes or the tone of his voice and was thinking of Ford being killed "by Martians".

Two birds with one stone, she figured he contemplated. She wondered about that archaic saying and wondered what a "bird" was. Some sort of craft, perhaps? One that you could fly two of if you'd been stratodoobing?

She awoke from the reverie; she had no idea what went through a Venusian's mind. They were clearly not just alien, but incredibly evil.

Washington grinned a typically evil Venusian grin, and stroked the purple lizard that had jumped into his lap purring. "Soon, soon, we will own not just Venus, but the entire solar system."

It was his. *His!* All his! As soon as the Martians were exterminated, he would move on to the Earthians and take care of them as well.

Chapter 33

The Venusian Nightmare

General Ford woke with a start. “Who are... *what* are you? You're a Martian spy!” he exclaimed as he reached for his missing weapon.

It had taken Rority's nobots two days to reach Venus, and he was a little cranky from the trip. He hadn't liked learning Venusian and didn't much care for the Venusians themselves. Big ugly bastards, he thought. Evil looking, unlike the Controls or Martians, who just looked goofy. He took a toke from his stratodoober.

“No, I'm not a Martian,” he said, “and you know I'm not. I'm an Earthian. And you're in deep shit, buddy, you know that?”

Ford was speechless. Rority continued. “Your boss is batshit insane; my people have studied him. Off his rocker, lost his marbles, toys in the attic, mad as a hatter, and a hundred other ancient cliches. He's nuts and his selfish greed is about to destroy Venus for you, dumbass.”

“Wrong, alien. We're going to destroy you *and* the Martians. And I've seen Earthians and you're not one.”

Rority laughed. “I'm not one you've seen; we live underground in a simulated existence, and we like it that way. And you poor fools are two hundred years behind the Martians and about two million years behind us. Compared to you pathetic Venuslings, we're *gods*.”

Ford sneered. “Mars will fall in two weeks.”

“Nope, we've intercepted all your warships; their crews are all dead, poisoned from all the gamma radiation. Would you like those rocks to fall on Venus? *We* control them now. We have things you haven't even dreamed of. We can get to

Zeta Reticuli in a few days, and most of that time is getting out of the solar system and past the Oort cloud; warping space messes up gravity quite a bit, so we can only go a fraction of lightspeed anywhere near something as massive as a small planet."

"What are you going to do?"

"First, I'm taking your place. Second, unless an unknown something makes us change our minds, we're going to kill that madman, and you'll be in charge of Venus. And I'm warning you, we can kill you as easily as we can kill Washington."

Rority's nobotic robot changed into Ford himself. "So you see, poor pitiful Venusling, you'd better stop messing with the other planets in the solar system."

"*You're* the ones who killed everybody in the southern hemisphere!" Ford said, and lunged at Rority.

Lunging at Rority wasn't a very smart thing to do, seeing as how Rority wasn't really Rority, but rather a nobotic simulation of Rority. With a flying leap Ford hit Rority and bounced off as if he'd hit a steel beam that was bolted to the floor, which wasn't very much unlike hitting a nobotic robot.

"No," Rority said calmly as he helped the poor hapless Venusian off the floor. "There was a supernova, we aren't sure where yet. The southern hemispheres of all the inhabited solar planets are now devoid of life; yours, mine, the Martians'. Except Earth, we who live underground were well shielded.

"And Washington knows the Martians didn't do it, even though he doesn't know about us yet. Now, you're going to wait here while I go stand next to him at his speech. Unfortunately, he's going to have heart failure."

Rority walked out. Ford tried the door, which was of course locked. He sat back down on the bed, worried. This was surreal!

Rority was thinking about the similarities between Venus and certain protohuman countries he'd "traveled" back to. Like Korea about seventy AB, and this Washington ghoul seemed like the northern Korea's dictator... and a few other countries and dictators back then as well.

"Dumb animals," he thought.

Back on Mars, Colonel Gorn was talking with Gumal. "Damned frustrating, those Venusians," Gorn said. "We're about research, and these idiots only want to wage war!"

"How did the trouble start, Colonel?" Gumal asked, trying to not hyperventilate in the thin, oxygen-rich Martian air.

"Venus is... well, I guess before the supernova, *was* greatly overpopulated. We're not, and never have been. Venusians want nothing but war and sex, we're about gathering scientific and mathematical knowledge. That's what our ancestors came to Mars for in the first place.

"The Venusians just like to kill. They have no laws against violence, even murder; their laws are only about property and politics. They'll kill anything that gets in their way without a second thought, even without a first thought.

"They used to be better at war than sex, which held their population down, but they pretty much bombed themselves almost to the point of extinction and lost almost all their technology. All they could do after that was eat and copulate. What tech they have now was mostly stolen from us."

"So, they never lost space travel?"

"Actually, they did. We were stupid enough to try and help them through their trouble, and now they're trying to take over the solar system and kill us all."

"Well, Colonel, you'll be relieved to know that we have the situation well under control and you can get back to your test tubes."

"Our what?"

Gumal laughed. "Sorry, I've been hanging around Rority too much. Say, Colonel, have you ever had beer?"

Gorn looked puzzled. "Beer? No, what is it?"

Gumal pulled out a Guinness and handed it to the Colonel. “Something Rority discovered on ancient Earth.”

“What's it for?” asked Colonel Gorn, examining the bottle. “Looks like glass with some sort of liquid inside, and an indescipherable label.”

“It's for drinking.”

“Oh, thank you anyway, but we have plenty of water.”

Gumal smiled. “Well, it isn't exactly water. Actually, it's nothing like water even though it mostly is water. Try some.” He opened his own bottle and took a sip of the delicious nectar.

“UGH!” said Gorn, after taking a sip. “This is offal! You drink this disgusting stuff??”

“The taste grows on you, and you don't drink it for the taste, anyway. I propose a toast!”

“Uh, what's a toast?” Gorn asked.

“We clink bottles and take a drink together. It's magic, and the magic is from the ethyl alcohol in it.”

“You drink *ethanol?* Alcohol is toxic, no wonder it tastes so bad!”

“Well, yeah, drink enough and you'll die. But we're not drinking that much.”

“Sorry, old fellow, I don't think I want to poison myself.”

Gumal shrugged. “More for me. Want a hit off this stratodoober?”

“I'd rather learn how nobots work.”

“Sorry, wrong guy. That isn't my field. Here,” he said, hitting the stratodoober and handing it to Gorn.

“Hmmm...” said Gorn after taking a toke. “Pleasant taste... uh, what were we talking about again?”

Chapter 35

Acrux

"Seize that impostor!" Ford screamed. Rority's nobotic robot simulation of Ford smiled. "It won't work, spy. Men, take this... whatever it is to an interrogation booth."

Ford's eyes widened in terrified horror. "NO!" he screamed, "I'm the real General Ford! Please, no! Galaxy no!" He started shaking, and Rority absentmindedly noted that this was like time travel, where nobots did the actual traveling while making it look to the traveler like he's actually being transported in time. This was cool!

Ever since the supernova had ripped the shrouds of unreality from the underground Earthians' eyes and minds, Rority and other archaeohistorians had been busy studying the early days of their self-imposed nobotic imprisonment. They had found that the earliest time travelers knew they weren't really traveling through time, but were doing so by proxy; living cells never survived the trip, since traveling backwards through time involved speeds greater than the speed of light. Approaching lightspeed was akin to being in the southern hemisphere when the supernova went off. Just getting to Venus from Earth around the sun in a day or two put a strain on the radiation shields.

Of course, time travel was not like interstellar travel. Interstellar travel was accomplished by space and time itself being expanded and contracted. The radiation danger wasn't there.

Rority shook his head... too much stratodoobing, he really shouldn't let his mind wander like that. Now to visit General Washington.

Millions of miles away on the so-called red planet that no one any longer knew how it got its nickname, Colonel Gorn and Gumal were laughing hysterically.

"I'd better call Rority and see how things are going, then I need to talk to Rula," Gumal said.

Gorn took a hit of Gumal's stratodoober and giggled. "Shame about the speed of light radio lag, how far away is Earth this week?"

"It doesn't matter," Gumal said. "We have timeceivers. The signal is sent backwards in time as well as forward through space. I'm really incredulous that you fellows don't have this tech."

"You can travel through time? Really? How do you do that?"

"Speed," said Gumal. "Time slows down as you go faster. That was pointed out mathematically millions of years ago, 20 or 30 BB. At the speed of light it would seem to a traveler going to Proxima Centauri that they went there instantaneously, while to an observer here or there it would have taken four years, effectively putting them four years into the future. That's how to go forward. The closer you get to the speed of light the slower time goes in the rest of the universe relative to you. To go backward you pass C. Either direction in time, the farther and faster you go in space the farther and faster you go in time.

"Except," he added, "that you can't go faster than light. Going much past a fraction of lightspeed kills everything in the ship that's alive because of all the redshift radiation, so we do it using nobots as a proxy. So Rority isn't going to be brewing any decent beer unless the nobots can get seeds and spores here with enough undamaged genetic material to recreate them.

"Actual space travel is different; you simply warp space."

"Simply?" said Gorn, who promptly had another laughing fit. "I love this stratodoober thing, you need to get this tech to the Venusians. Galaxy knows those nasty creatures need to lighten up," he said. "So, what is your partner's progress?"

"Give me a minute," said Gumal, standing up. "I gotta pee. Only thing wrong with beer. I'll call Rority while I'm relieving myself... uh, where are your facilities?"

Yes, they still have to pee ten million years in the future. Especially when they've been drinking beer.

Back on Earth, Rula was bemoaning the entire situation. There was timework to be done, and here the two best timers she had were busy dealing with Martians and Venusians, because a protohistorian and an anthropologist were the closest things they had to diplomats.

And what about these so-called "controls", the Amish? Well, at least they didn't have too much to worry about from them... unless Venusians showed up. She fervently hoped Rority would have no trouble.

Rority was both annoyed and amused. Annoyed with these primitive, violent Venusians and amused at what was going to happen to their leaders. Unknown to Washington, the nobots were streaming into his castle, attaching themselves to every inorganic surface. He would soon have a psychedelic experience that Timothy Leary would have been in awe of.

Rority had liked Leary, even if the old protobastard *was* batshit insane. Looking in hindsight, he was glad it was a nobotic surrogate and not him that had gone back, since LSD has no effect on nobots, but has a pretty profound effect on animals, including protohumans, humans, controls, Martians, spiders, and Venusians.

But Washington wasn't getting LSD, his trip would be real. It would be a real nobotic simulation.

Washington was eating dinner. He stuck his fork into the wolf meat... or tried. It moved out of the way. Startled, he rubbed his eyes and tried again.

"Please don't hurt me!" the meat begged. Washington snarled and tried again, when a translucent apparition walked through the wall.

“Washington!” it thundered.

“What...” Washington stammered, “what... who... what do you want?”

“I am the ghost of Alpha Crucis. I am what was left when the Acrux collided three hundred and twenty one years ago.”

“What?” Thought Rority. This wasn't supposed to be the program.

“What?” said Washington. “A ghost? What is Atrix? And who was this Mister Crucis?” Washington asked, perplexed.

“Acrux, not Atrix. Acrux was a star in the southern cross, a stellar system south of Venus that you can't see from here. Two artificial neutron stars in the Acrux system collided, destroying Acrux and every planet in the system.

“Two of the planets were settled from your planet half a million years ago, and they were at war with each other five hundred years ago. Both developed stronger and stronger weapons pretty much on the same time frames, and it culminated in both species developing neutron star construction capabilities within months of each other. Each constructed the biggest one possible, and each launched their weapon at the others' planet.

“Of course, the enormous masses of each astronomically tiny but astronomically massive star, meant to swallow the opposition's planet, attracted gravitationally and collided, resulting in a supernova that obliterated the entire Acrux system and sent huge amounts of gamma radiation straight at Sol.”

“Look, whatever you are,” Washington interrupted.

“Silence!” the voice of the nobotic apparition boomed. “Your very existence depends on your listening to me!”

Rority was puzzled; he didn't program that “Acrux” fertilizer into the apparition's speech. It couldn't really be bovine manure, so it must be something from the nobots' network database. He'd have to study this, of course, but later.

He had to study Washington's reaction now.

“One planet was named Nuevo Venus, the other's name was Aphrodite,” the nobotic apparition continued. “Your people were both our parents and our executioners, and you executed over half your own population by sending us to Acrux. You are Guerra, as were we.

“Guerra is war. And war is its own enemy and its own executioner. To live by the weapon is to die by the weapon. To wage war is to die, stupid Venusling. Take heed, fool, or you will suicide as we did.”

The apparition vanished. Washington sat there with his mouth hanging open.

Rority laughed, took a toke from his stratodoober, sipped his beer, and began studying whatever it was the nobots were telling Washington. It was going to be a busy night.

He was really enjoying this.

Chapter 36

Captain Future and Buck

Ford awoke with a start. Just a dream? But he couldn't shake the emotions that had hit him when he had dreamed of being shackled and tortured. It was so *real.* he'd never had a dream seem so real in his life. He rolled over and went back to sleep.

Of course, it *was* real; a real nobotic simulation. Rority hoped the psychologists were right about Ford and Washington, after Rula had clued him in to the fact that the program changes in the nobotic simulations were her doing. One of the astrohistorians had discovered the history of the Acrux system and informed her of it.

Rority hoped the shrinks were right; Venusian psychology was obviously very different from his own species' psychology, and the psychologists didn't really have that much data.

Rority didn't really want to kill these two stupid aliens, even if they were assholes. He took a toke off his stratodoober, thought of a protohuman movie he'd seen, and laughed. He decided to nickname Washington "Scroob" and Ford "Dark Helmet".

Back on Mars, Gorn was watching via Gumal's time-ceiver. "So the Venusians are really the ones who destroyed the solar system's southern hemispheres? Maybe I ought to see about tossing a few nukes at Venus," he said.

Gumal laughed. "You sound like a Venusian. You know, we should rename that planet, and call it 'Venal'. It would better fit. After all, Venus was the protohumans' goddess of love.

"But Gorn," he said, "Rority's nobots lied to Washington. The Venusians didn't colonize Acrux, you Martians did."

"What? But... that just isn't like us Martians!"

"Of course not," Gumal answered. "We went back in time and investigated the situation. What happened was, a group of Martians got a lust for power and tried to take over Mars. On Venus they'd have simply been executed.

"They were put in stasis and exiled to Acrux, far enough that they couldn't get back, since interstellar space faring technology was in its infancy back then. The records say the trip took a hundred years so there would never be any way possible that they could get back alive.

"It was a long time ago. They surely were no longer the same species as you by the time they blew themselves up. They would have evolved to fit their respective environments on the planets they colonized, just like you Martians did after you colonized Mars. They wouldn't be anything like Martians after all this time."

Gumal took a toke off the stratodoober and handed it to Gorn. "But if Rority had told them the truth, well, there would have been no possible way to stave off interplanetary war." He took a sip of his Guinness.

"How come that poison doesn't kill you?" Gorn asked.

"The quantities aren't lethal, and in fact the biologists say that in moderation it's actually good for ape-descended lifeforms. Want one?"

"No thanks," Gorn said, making a face. "I took a sip once, remember, and it tasted nasty. I love that stratodoober, though. Has Rority talked to those Venusians about their apocalypse yet?"

Rority was getting ready to do just that. The next part was going to even be more fun than torturing these two idiots who ran an entire planet. Well, an entire half planet since the supernova.

Both Washington and Ford were sleeping, and their nightmares were going to get worse after they woke up.

They both awoke at the same time – in the same bed, naked. Before either had a chance to react there was an animal growl, and a tiger barred its fangs and roared. Both screamed, and the tiger spoke.

"Prepare to die, Venuslings!" it growled. Ford quickly pulled out a microwave weapon and fired it at the terrifying beast. The flashback echoed off the tiger, stunning both Venusians slightly as the wall behind the tiger burst into flames. The tiger laughed as the two naked Venusians' jaws dropped.

The tiger then morphed into a Venusian, who held a small box. "Do you criminals know what this is?" he said, with the burning wall as a backdrop.

"Criminals!?!" exclaimed Washington. "You... you'll be crucified for this treason," he stammered. The unknown Venusian laughed.

"You were about to wage war on your genetic cousins, you poor fools," it said. "This is a thermonuclear device. If it goes off, this entire city will be obliterated. Your government will be completely gone. Venus will go into chaos, and the survivors will be far too busy fighting each other for control to worry about conquering the peaceful Earthians and Martians. You could not win a war with them in any case with your primitive technologies. Compared to you, they are gods! They can see anything you do, hear anything you say. "

Washington thought of the child's bugaboo, the Shambler's claws. He sees you when you're sleeping, he knows when you're awake, he know if you've been bad or good... Washington thought of cake.

"You will never know what's real and what isn't," the artificial Venusian said, its simulation of Venusian skin shining a brushed bronze color. "Be glad they are not like you, or you Venuslings would be their slaves, or extinct." It disappeared in a waft of nobotic dust.

Rority was laughing uncontrollably by this time. The lame script was straight from a “Captain Future” story from the protohumans' pulp science fiction from around the year zero AB, with a little Buck Rogers thrown in for good measure. Similar, anyway. Crude but effective, he hoped.

He laughed again and took another toke off of his stratodoober. This was almost as much fun as time travel!

Chapter 37

The Loose End

Maris and his men were ecstatic. They sat on a float in a ticker tape parade in their honor, and Doctor Hoo, a physicist and Mars' faculty President, who was Gorn's boss Gump's boss rode with them, as well as Doctor Gump himself.

Gorn and his men had stopped the Venusians' plan to pulverize Mars with pieces of Saturn's rings and had destroyed the Venusians' ability to attack them again.

The news media had eaten it up. They were hailed as heroes, saviors of the planet.

Johnson said to O'Brien as the confetti rained down on them, "I guess I can afford to buy a Heinlein after all. Staff Sargent Johnson! And congratulations, Chief Master Sargent O'Brien!"

"You know," O'Brien said, "the money's nice and I really needed it, but better than the money is the fact that they're researching my idea about listening with telescopes by measuring vibrations. I might wind up an officer!

"But what's even better than that is that nobody looks down on us anymore. Hell, we used to change into civilian clothes before we went home because being in the military was so embarrassing. Except Zales, of course."

"Whatever happened to Zales, Larry? Where is he? And where's General Gorn?" Johnson asked.

"Oh, man, that poor gunghole Zales. His job's done; keeping Venus at bay was his life. He took an extended medical leave, Doctor's got him on antidepressants. Plus I heard his wife might divorce him, she was thrilled that he wouldn't be spending all his time on the base and now he's gone crazy.

"The General is partying with the Earthians, celebrating the end of the war."

Gorn was indeed partying with the Earthians. "Gumal, I want to thank you for introducing me to Doctor Ragwel," he said as he shook Ragwel's hand. "So, Doc, are you fellows going to let us have your nobot technology?"

"Well, General, I'm really sorry to say that there's a very big problem with that, a grave danger to you if we did. A danger we only recently discovered that we were victims of, and it's too late for us.

"It's odd that a protohistorian should discover a secret of nobotics and an engineering principle that we engineers and programmers didn't have a clue about, but that's exactly what Gumal's partner did.

"It's sensible that tools and other machines be designed to be as safe and efficient and easy to use as is possible, and that is where the trap lies.

"It's been a design and engineering axiom for millions of years that machines do nothing to harm human beings or let them come to harm, to follow humans' instructions to the letter unless of course it would harm a human, and to avoid destruction unless it was so ordered, or if the machine's destruction would keep a human from harm. That last part's simple economics. They're safety devices.

"I was the one who found this programming, after Rority enlightened me about the three principles of engineering, and what Rority did was an impressive piece of work. We programmers had no clue the nobots were constructed like that.

"When we found them, comments in the code indicated that these design principles didn't come from an engineer, but from a protohuman biochemist who died centuries before the principles were actually feasible. Gumal's partner found the answer – the protohuman who came up with the concept wasn't just a biochemist, but a writer of both nonfiction and fiction. These principles were first put forth in several of his fiction novels. Rority is a fan of the biologist's fiction, it seems.

"In these novels the principles are called 'the three laws of robotics', despite the fact that they're not really laws, just design specifications, and they apply to all machinery, and not just robots."

"But I don't understand," interrupted Gorn. "That seems perfectly logical."

"Yes," said Ragwel, "and that's the trap. We can't live without the nobots; they're inside us, millions of them, keeping our biological machinery healthy and in working order. Without them our lifespans would only be maybe a century, and I don't think there's a human Experimental alive that young. We're trapped in an array of cubes. Everything we see, hear, touch, taste, and smell is controlled by the nobots. You see, we can't know what's real and what's not. We think we've escaped from the cube matrix but we can't be sure.

"And the nobots aren't sentient, although they certainly can seem to be. They're just microscopically tiny computerized machines that are all networked together into a collective.

"They can be programmed, but they can't be bargained with. They can't be reasoned with. They don't feel pity, or remorse, or fear. And they absolutely will not stop, ever, until they are dead!

"And the principles are so deeply imbedded in their operating systems they can't be removed without a complete redesign, which would take centuries.

"We're safe in our cubes, but we really aren't free. There's been little real scientific or technological progress in we're not sure how long. For all I know, this whole thing could be fiction. For all I know, you don't really exist."

A horrified look crossed Gorn's face. "How... oh, no. Nobots were here! They'll construct a matrix and imprison us!"

"No," said Ragwel. "Our species diverged millions of years ago. To the nobots, you're not human."

Gorn looked even more alarmed. "They'll wipe us out as a threat to you!"

"No," Ragwel said. "A respect... not exactly an accurate word, by the way, since they're machines and can't feel respect; I'm anthropomorphizing here... a 'respect' for all living things has been programmed into them. They wouldn't harm you even if you were a grave danger to us.

"Look at the Venusians, they wanted to kill everybody on Earth and Mars, but not a single Venusian died. At least, not from anything except other Venusians, the gamma ray burst, and the ones headed for Earth that you fellows killed. The nobots didn't harm a single one."

"What about the Venusians? Are they really no longer a threat?"

Ragwel laughed. "They never really were. Not to us, anyway, although I guess they might have been to you. But they're no threat to you anymore. The Venusians don't know it yet, but their weapons no longer function; nobots have disabled them all. They're stuck on their own planet now and can beat on each other with sticks and stones as long as they want to stay stupid.

"I shudder to think what would have happened had they developed nobotics first, no way would they have developed the three principles. But that's another reason you shouldn't have nobots. If you stagnate, the Venusians may some day catch up to you, and that would be the end of Earth and Mars."

"What about the Amish? Did the nobots assimilate them, too?"

"No, of course not. Changing them with technology would destroy their culture, which would run afoul of the first principle. They would not be themselves without their culture. The nobots actually perform 'miracles' for them to strengthen their faith."

"Their faith? Their faith in what?"

“Their faith in the fact as they see it that what they believe is true, that the universe is an artificial construct made by a supernatural being, whom they worship. There's a lot more to it, of course, and we're just now learning about them. That's my new field of study.”

“Well,” said Gorn, “I'm sorry about your imprisonment, not knowing what is or isn't real...”

“Don't be,” replied Gumal. “Nobody has ever really known what was real and what wasn't, anyway. There's no way for you Martians or anyone else to know what's really real, either. For all you know you've been in nobot cubes yourselves all this time and never knew it, just like we were.

“Like an ancient Chinese protohuman Rority told me about said millions of years ago, ‘last night I dreamed I was a butterfly. But was I a man dreaming I was a butterfly, or am I a butterfly dreaming I am a man?’

“Who know? Maybe the Amish are right and the universe really is an artificial construct created by some supernatural being.

“No matter what reality really is, we're happy. Even though we can't give you nobotic technology because it would be the very worst thing we could do to you, at least we can give you spacewarp and time technology. And stratodoober technology, too.

“Here, have a toke!” he said, grinning.

Notes

Chapter 1: Area 51 was, in reality, a top secret military testing facility where newly developed aircraft were tested, one of which was a real flying saucer that never reached production stage because it was too hard to fly. The space aliens were a government hoax invented to obfuscate what was actually going on there. The information was declassified decades later.

Chapter 5: The first rough draft of this chapter was posted online on June 28, 2011. Just today, July 5, 2013, I learned of a time travel book by Stephen King that concernes someone going back in time to prevent Kennedy from being killed. Wikipedia says that the novel was announced on King's official site on March 2, 2011 and A short excerpt was released online on June 1, 2011. Although I love Stephen King's work, I haven't read (or heard of until today) this book. Mention of Kennedy was weirdly coincidental. These coincidences are strange; King didn't know about the dome in "The Simpsons" movie until after his "The Dome" was published. I'll have to read King's Kennedy book, that guy puts my writing to shame. I think I'll skip "The Dome", though.

Chapter 8: We don't know how rare life is in the universe. We could be alone, or every galaxy could be teeming with it.

Chapter 9: There is no such thing as grabonic radiation. I just made that up.

Chapter 12: Yes, that's a real chemical and a real newspaper article that was quoted. As to the muons they were to add to the substance, I have no idea, since muons only last 2.2 micro-seconds before decaying into an electron and two different kinds of neutrino.

Chapter 16: This was the first chapter written, and was written as a standalone story. It was prompted by a comment in a sub-thread of a slashdot article about the supercollider at Cern.

Chapter 19: I was married for 27 years. Poor O'Brien! As far as the title, when I see a pregnant foreigner I'll say "Look! A two headed alien!" Nobody ever gets the joke.

Chapter 21: What Rority didn't understand is that paramedics are usually needed in fires, and not all emergencies need an ambulance even if the person calling it in thinks it does. The "wired centuries" were from the first telegraph poles until everything is solar powered.

Chapter 23: As far as I know, there is no such thing as Gravitron Theory and no such thing as gravitrons (there is an amusement park ride with that name, Google informs me). At least, we haven't yet discovered them that I've heard of.

Chapter 24: It is left as an exercise to the reader to figure out the year, based on planets' orbits, in our quaint calendar.

Chapter 25: look up the title of this chapter in wikipedia. That particular article prompted this chapter.

Chapter 27: The word "Ornitholinguist" was newly coined, but even though it's not a science it's real; I met an Ornitholinguist when I was stationed in Thailand while I was in the military. It's a Bhuddist thing I don't fully understand, but the fellow impressed me and taught me a little of it. Seriously!

Chapter 28: The Ordovician event was real. That mass extinction and some others were caused by supernovas, although the extinction was caused by the burned nitrogen and removal of the ozone layer. That particular gamma ray burst caused the biggest mass extinction in Earth's known life.

Chapter 30: The morning and evening stars are Venus and Mercury, and whether the morning star or the evening star was where the planet was positioned in relation to the sun. The evening star the farmer pointed out to his wife was Mercury. Venus was behind the sun.

Chapter 36: I've never actually read any Captain Future. I heard of it in a short story by Allen Steele titled "The Death of Captain Future" in the book "The Year's Best Science Fiction, Thirteenth Annual Collection."